To
Karen
and
Bill

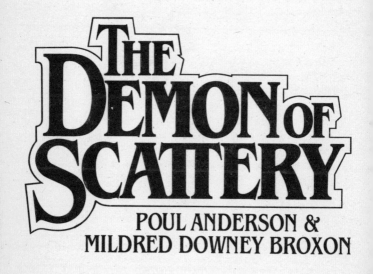

THE DEMON OF SCATTERY

POUL ANDERSON & MILDRED DOWNEY BROXON

SF
ace books

A Division of Charter Communications Inc.
A GROSSET & DUNLAP COMPANY
360 Park Avenue South
New York, New York 10010

THE DEMON OF SCATTERY

An ACE Book

Cover art by Michael Whelan

Text design by Grace Markman

First Ace printing: December 1979
First Mass Market Printing: June 1980

2 4 6 8 0 9 7 5 3 1
Manufactured in the United States of America

Once in the war between elves and trolls, it happened that Skafloc fled England to seek help among the Sídhe. He was a mortal who had been fostered by elvenkind; he bore with him the halves of the sword called Tyrfing. Could that weapon be forged anew, it would bring victory to his folk. They were in sore plight. But no smith could mend it save Bolverk, the blind giant afar in Jötunheim.

Mananaan MacLir befriended Skafloc in Ireland, and they set sail together on the quest. Though their boat was small, her hull and rigging were charged with the force of Mananaan, who had been a god before the White Christ came, and who was still a might to reckon with on deep water. Also, at the prow danced the figurehead of Fand his lady.

Farther northward the twain fared than a man-built ship would have gone before making landfall. Darkness lit by aurora fell over the sea.

Icebergs went like moving mountains; from them welled frost. Strange beings prowled half-seen around the strakes. Again and again must Mananaan strain to the utmost his powers over wind and wave.

Yet even on the hardest passage, times will come when seamen find naught to do but sit and spin yarns. It staves off the loneliness.

Thus Mananaan, at ease on a bench, regarded Skafloc, who held the rudder. Tall was Mananaan and fair to see, with clear features, greenish-gold locks, and eyes that held the changeable hues of ocean. His green cloak, white tunic, golden torque and armlets bore the only bright colors within the rim of sight. He strummed a harp as he said, low and slow:

"My friend, you are steering toward more than you know. You steer toward your fate, and what that might be I cannot tell. Yours is the blood of strangers; what burdens you is not the *geas* my people know. Now the world and the halfworld are changing, and I think all Faerie lies under an unforeseeable doom.

"Even so, from what was, we can draw some understanding of what is, and perhaps of what shall be. I am thinking on a thing that happened in Ireland near a hundred years ago. Kindred of yours were caught in it, and at the end even I played a part. What it all meant lies outside my ken. I wonder if any god knows what really happened, unless he be too great for me to speak with.

"But told from the human side, the tale can be followed. It may enlighten you in some way. If not, it may at least pass a few hours of our voyage."

I

The vikings reached Scattery Island on the
first of April. This was a day of cold winds off the
sea, noise and spray in the air, clouds at whose
hasty shadows the sun cast spears. Whitecaps
chopped across the Shannon mouth and the
river itself ran darkling. New leaves tossed in the
woods along either bank; spring green rippled
over plowlands. Smoke blew in rags from the

farmsteads yonder, but Halldor made out no folk
and few kine. Everybody must have fled when
the ships hove in sight.

No. On the holm before him, the monks straggled from their chapel, milled briefly about like
ants whose nest has been trampled, and ran for
the tower. They had only one or two small cur-
raghs, which could ferry but few of them away in
time, and he had caught them unready, at their
devotions. Norse dragons swam fast. Besides,
the monks had their church treasures to ward,
and a stout place wherein to stand siege.

From the tiller of his craft, Halldor gazed
down its crowded length to his goal. He had
ordered the sail struck and oars out. Forty men,
two to a shaft, cast their strength into the work,
and *Sea Bear* drove forward with her hull
a-shiver. Some chanted together to help keep the
beat, *"Tyr hold us, ye Tyr, ye Odin"* hoarse
amidst thole-creak, wave-splash, rig-thrum of a
mast not yet unstepped. Helmets gleamed on
their heads, ringmail on the shoulders of those
who owned it. Proud on the foredeck as lookout,
shining in iron, Halldor's son Ranulf laid hand
on the snarling beast-head mounted at the prow.

His father's glance dropped, and brows drew
into a scowl. A woman knelt in the hull below
Ranulf's feet. Though cowl and flapping cloak
covered most of her, Halldor saw clasped hands
and knew she was calling on her White Christ—
in a whisper, but it might reach far. He touched
the small silver hammer at his throat and drew

Thor's sign.

The steering oar bucked, to let him know it wanted his full grasp. He shrugged off his faint misgivings. Her saints and angels had helped her naught when the Norsemen sacked her convent some days agone and Ranulf ran her down across a field. Indeed, she was the only one who was taken away, he and some of his friends finding her sightly enough to be worth her keep out of their shares of food and drink . . . for a while, at least.

Halldor turned his mind toward the other two ships, Arrow-Egil's gaudy *Reginleif* and Sigurd Tryggvason's *Shark*. Good, they were still where he wanted them, aft of his to starboard and larboard. He hadn't been sure of that, for although their skippers and he had sworn brotherhood, they had merely agreed to follow his redes as long as they deemed those to be sound.

Several more had called him over-careful. He was a fine seaman, they admitted, but no viking. He had not let himself get angry. It was true; he was a trader, raiding not because he wanted to but because he must. He had answered mildly that he had not kept himself alive through five and forty winters by using his head only for a hat rest.

This had been in Armagh, in the north of Ireland, where a number of crews were lying over between fall and spring rather than go back to Norway. . . .

Halldor had been asking everyone about the western coast; he had learned Irish several years earlier. At last he had fared thither on horseback with a few trusty companions. To those he met along the way, he said he was a messenger; but he always looked about him, and beheld the richness of the land. On his return, Egil and Sigurd were ready to listen. They were from Thrandheim too and knew him of old.

The three sat in a wattle-and-daub hut. Eye-smarting smoke drifted thick below the thatch. From the rafters hung meat the farmwife had set to cure before she and her family were driven off. Rain pattered on the roof and lay pooled outside the wicker door.

"Pickings ought to be good along the lower Shannon," Halldor said. "Our folk have not been that way in a long time. Farmsteads, monasteries, churches with their golden vessels—all lie waiting for us. Of course, others besides me know this. We should start early, to arrive first. From the way the season has gone thus far, we might safely embark a little before the equinox."

They were somewhat surprised, but took him at his word. He was not called Halldor the Weatherwise for nothing; throughout his life he had paid close heed to sea and sky, and thought much about what he saw.

Sigurd did frown and say, "Um-m-m, we'll be just three shipsful. Man for man, the Irish fight as well as our own lads. If a chieftain there-abouts can quickly gather a host, we might have a nasty surprise."

"Halldor, of all men, has surely planned against that," Egil answered.

However well meant, his words smote painfully. During the past summer, the second he spent in viking, Halldor had been ambushed ashore and lost Ivar, the older of his two living sons. Soon afterward, Ranulf had arrived from home in his father's trading vessel, ablaze with the wish to leave sixteen years of boyhood behind him.

"I have," Halldor said as steadily as might be. "We want a base that we can hold against attack. Not that I reckon it likely we'll be set on in force. However, it's well to be ready. It's also well to have a place where we can rest in safety, tend our ships and gear, maybe share out the plunder if it's ample—for you know I want to end this cruise as soon as I've piled up what wealth I need." He drained his beer horn and beckoned through the murk of the hut for a thrall to bring him more. "Spying," he said, "I've found the right spot, too: an eyot settled by none but Papas."

"Christian kirkfolk? Good!" More than greed roughened Egil's voice. Like many Norsemen, he saw witchcraft and bad luck in a faith that scorned all other gods.

—And so, while the last winter winds howled—but less mightily than usual, as Halldor had foretold—they had set forth west and then south along Ireland, raiding as they

went. At first, not much was left for them. Later they struck an untouched convent, but it yielded scant loot. Now, soon after, they had turned into the great river and were approaching Scattery Island. . . .

The clangor of a bell, blown downwind to his ears, roused Halldor from those flitting memories. That near had he come, rounding a spit at the north end to seek the sheltered bay on the east side. A half mile to larboard was lesser Hog Island; the nearer shore of the mainland lay as far again beyond. The sound loudened with every leap of his craft: clearly from a big bell, whose bronze would fetch a hefty price in Norway. The peals cried out of the tower which loomed over Scattery. Heaven whistled and scudded around it.

Entering the bay, he squinted in search of the best ground, for there was no dock. Crow's-feet wrinkles deepened around light blue eyes in a broad, high-cheeked, broken-nosed face. Grizzled yellow hair and close-cropped beard glistened with spindrift. The hauberk clashed on his burly frame when he leaned hard against the tiller.

Scattery was itself small, about a mile long north-and-south, half a mile wide, low-lying in the water. Trees along the western rim were a shield-wall against storms for wattle-and-daub huts and a tiny stone church huddled not far from the strand. Otherwise he made out garden

plots, grass and wildflowers beyond—and, near
the church, the round tower. Of grey stone, skill-
fully dry-laid, that thing reared a hundred feet or
more to its conical slate roof. Windows stared
from each floor like sockets in the skull of a saint.
The wooden door was ten feet aloft, reached by a
ladder which the monks had pulled after them.

The vikings rowed slower now, until shingle
grated beneath *Sea Bear*'s keel. Ranulf was the
first overside. *"Yuk-hei-saa-saa!"* he screamed,
the old battle yell. None of the warriors who had
stood to their weapons and straightway followed him said aught, for nobody was here to
fight. Oarsmen drew the sweeps inboard,
dropped them clashing amidst the benches, took
up their stowed arms, and likewise jumped. Had
foes been on hand, Halldor would have been in
the lead. As was, he could make fast the rudder,
out of harm's way, before he too sought the bow
and sprang.

The Irishwoman, Brigit, was kneeling there
abaft the foredeck. Beyond her he glimpsed the
real hammer he kept in its rack, hallowed to
Thor. A horror too great for weeping was upon
her. He made out words she stammered in her
own tongue. "—Easter Sunday, and the heathen
come to the holy isle—Easter—*Eli, Eli, lamach
sabachthani?*" He didn't understand that last.

No matter. He leaped. The water belted his
waist, chill and swift. No shield encumbered his
wading ashore, for he wielded an ax. While he
helped draw the ship well up, he saw the Irish-

woman rise. She straightened her back and waved at the tower. He liked that.

Shark and *Reginleif* neared. Halldor signalled them to come in, the ground being shown safe for good-sized hulls. "Let's go, let's go!" Ranulf cried.

"Stay," his father said. "They'll not run away yonder." The lad dithered all the while that the rest of the Norsemen came to land, made fast their vessels, posted guards, and formed a band to move on toward the tower.

At a shout from Halldor they came to a halt beyond bowshot of that stronghold. A few arrows nonetheless flew from its windows. The waste and the short way they sped told him that nobody schooled in war was there.

He stepped ahead of his troop, with small fear of being hit by such archers, till he was almost at the wall. Staring along its height to the swiftness of clouds overhead, he felt as if it were toppling on him; his feet, wet and cold in their boots, curled toes toward firm earth. Gulls wheeled above, mewing through the wind.

He filled his lungs and shouted in Irish, "Ahoy, you! Will you be talking?"

After a short while, a man leaned out of a lower opening. Though the hair around his tonsure was white and he had not many teeth left, his call resounded: "Michael speaks, abbot of Saint Senan's. Are you Christian?"

"No, but I'm prime-signed." Halldor had undergone that rite years ago; by it he did not forswear his friend Thor, but he became one with whom the baptized might lawfully deal. "I've traded in England and France as well as Scotland and Ireland. They do not think ill there of Halldor Ketilsson."

"Those are no chapman's craft which bear you, those lean hulls with demon figureheads."

"Oh, we are in viking this time. However, I'm not the kind who'd slaughter needlessly. Yield, and all of you shall go free, yes, even the sturdy ones we could sell. I will swear this by any oath you wish, and by my own honor in the hearing of shipmates."

The abbot's gaunt frame stiffened yet further. "Think you in your pride that we, to save our poor lives, would let you profane the house of God, scatter the sacred vessels and relics, make the sanctuary a den of robbers?" He spat. Had the wind blown less strong, he might have struck his target. "And this on the very day when Christ is risen? We've meat and drink in here, and we're well-used to fasting. God will send us help."

"If you try to hold out, I can promise nothing," Halldor warned.

"What worth can be given a heathen's word? Rage, then, if you will. Slay us, and we fall as martyrs, who'll afterward watch from Heaven as you writhe in Hell." Michael caught his breath, mastered his fury, tempered his shout. "Beware, Lochlannach. This is most sacred ground that you tread. In ages past, Saint Senan banished a monster from here, a creature more

frightful by far than your flimsy dragon ships.
We keep his holy rule. He will not forsake us.
Beware, Lochlannach!"

Halldor had heard that legend when he was
spying in these parts, and thought little of it; he
had often met its kind. The abbot was merely,
forlornly seeking to daunt him by it. "Well, you
can still yield before we attack," the Norseman
offered, and walked off. Despite the poor
marksmanship of the defenders and the byrnie
which ought to turn their weakly driven arrows,
a tightness clutched between his shoulderblades
till he got back to his folk.

He had no wish to die. Whatever lay beyond—
in Norway alone, one heard of feasting in god-
halls, gloom in the nether depths, strange half-
life in the grave, rebirth, and who knew how

much else?—this world was his, friends and kindred, home and holdings, Unn his wife, their daughters who were lately wedded and beginning to bring forth grandchildren, the hope of the house that lay in Ranulf, the growth of a grainfield or a woodcarving beneath his hands, merriment, wide farings, endless play of sky, water, weather. . . .

—"Burn them out," Egil said. "Cut wood from the trees and those hovels, stack it around, put the torch to it."

"Hear them yell while they fry," Ranulf cackled.

Halldor frowned at his son and answered:

Stillness beseems the youthful.
Speak not with nothing to speak from.
That wolf will win the most meat
Which warily gangs after prey."

He was somewhat of a skald, and thought a stave was the mildest way to chide the boy—who flushed and withdrew, stiff-legged.

To Egil, Sigurd, and the rest in earshot, Halldor said, "Have you forgotten? We want that tower for ourselves, a safeguard. A fire would bring down the floors and make it useless. Also, steering in, did you not see the Papas shift their wealth there, whatever it is?"

"If their books burn, well and good," Egil snapped.

"I've handled books and come to no harm," Halldor told him. "Rather, I've learned things. It's a shame so many among us fear they hold baneful wizardry. But if naught else, what of embroidered cloth threaded with pearls and gold, or silver chalices, or crystal-studded boxes, that would be lost?"

"What, then, would you do?" Sigurd asked him.

"What I awaited from the start," Halldor said. "We knock together a framework to stand on, and bring it to the tower, and beat in the door. We'll need a ladder or two as well, inside, but not much else. Those hymn-singers can't do anything against us hand-to-hand."

He felt the least bit sorry for the monks. They were bearing themselves like men.

The afternoon was old when everything was ready. Halldor helped drag the scaffold to its place—the trunk of a young rowan, the shaft of a spare oar were cool and smooth against his palms—and was first up. On the way, arrows and flung stones dealt the vikings no more than a few flesh wounds, and made them hoot laughter.

When he swarmed aloft, the rungs were steady beneath his feet. Mostly the frame was held by lashings, but he had himself driven nails into key spots. Those he carried on *Sea Bear* for making repairs, and the hammer he used was Thor's.

It was his ax, though, which he now swung. Two fellows beside him on the platform did likewise. The blows thundered, splinters flew, gashes opened white, the door gave way. Beyond was a room bare and dim, a hole in its ceiling for

farther passage. The monks seemed to have gathered on top, just below the tower roof. Warriors pushed in around Halldor. They brought a ladder. He mounted. Their baying echoed back and forth. Beyond, he heard the bulk of his folk raven at the foot of the buildings like dogs at a tree wherein a squirrel is trapped.

The racket turned into a howl. Words cut through: *"They're dropping boulders–"* Wrath roared.

"I told everybody to stay clear of those windows," groaned Halldor. He could well-nigh see before him a heavy rock, gathering speed as it fell a hundred feet, smashing through iron and bone till brains spurted and a man crumpled. . . .

Egil overhauled him as he was about to climb from the fifth to the sixth floor. Behind shaggy red beard, below sea-leathered skin, the skipper of *Reginleif* shivered, swallowed, and could hardly speak: "Halldor, a stone struck Ranulf, your son. It stove in his helmet and—He breathes yet, but—"

It was eerie, thought a part of Halldor, that he did not feel at once what had happened. To turn and clamber back down was only a thing he did, like drawing breath. Deep wounds are slow to give pain.

He did stop caring what became of the monks. It would have been wise to keep some, at least, to question and to sell if they were healthy. As was, without him to forbid, the vikings slew them all.

II

Brigit watched the confrontation between monks and Lochlannach and saw how Halldor directed the construction of a ladder. She could do naught to help her countrymen. The strangers were too strong; well had she learned that. Instead she stole to the stone chapel, to seek there what solace she might. Days since she had stood in a sanctuary—

The chapel was cool and dim, and the scent of incense from Easter Mass yet hung in the air. The altar had been stripped of its treasures, she saw, and only a small oil lamp lit the gloom. She knelt on the earthen floor.

Outside she heard screams as the monks were slaughtered. She clasped her hands and bowed her head. "Oh great Lord God," she began. But since her capture her prayers were empty. Naught save her pride, now, kept her alive while Ranulf and his friends used her: her cursèd pride and her ability to dream her mind elsewhere. Her body was bruised and battered, but her soul stayed untouched. Or so she must believe.

A figure in the doorway blocked the light. Brigit looked up. Had they come at last to kill her? How she would welcome martyrdom.

The man before her bore no weapons; he carried a body in his arms. Its features were

bloodstained, but it wore Ranulf's armor.

For a moment Brigit was glad. A youth driven to prove his manhood, Ranulf was a cruel master. And he spoke no word of Gaelic, nor did his friends. She had fallen to the mercy of beasts. Perhaps Ranulf would die, or was already dead. No, such a thought was unChristian.

Then she saw who held the boy, and she snapped after breath. Halldor, captain of the lead ship—Ranulf's father! Twisted and terrible was his face, narrowed his deep-blue eyes. He carried his son as if the weight were an infant's.

"Your monks did this," he said in Gaelic. He strode toward the altar. "Clear that table."

Wordless, Brigit moved the wine and water cruets, a crucifix, and a bookstand. *God forgive me*, she cried into the emptiness.

Halldor laid his son out on the altar cloth and pulled off the dented helmet. Dark blood spilled from the wound. Ranulf yet breathed, Brigit saw, but slowly, as if death crouched on his chest. His skull was dented beneath his helm.

One of Halldor's men stepped forward and examined the wound. He pulled back Ranulf's eyelids, shook his head, and said something in Norse.

Halldor's reply was short. The other man spread his hands in a gesture of resignation. Halldor stood looking down at his son. Brigit saw tension in his shoulders. *Even if he is a barbarian, he is also a father, and he grieves*. Then, with practicality: *The procedure would be dif-*

*ficult, and nothing is sure. But the old Abbess
showed me a way, and if the son survives the father
should be grateful.*

Decision came, and with it, strength. She
stepped forward. "I was trained in leechcraft."

Halldor's eyes were full of misery. He looked
at her and raised his hand. She drew back, ex-
pecting a blow. Instead he let his arm fall. It
dangled useless at his side. "Then do what you
can, woman," he answered. "If Ranulf dies, so do
you."

If it's death I wished for, I've a fair chance to get my boon. But for the first time in days Brigit felt hope. "Dear God, guide my hands."

Her medicine bag—her *lés*—had been left behind, destroyed when the vikings sacked her convent, but surely the monks had numbered a leech among them. Whoever he was he would have no further use for his tools.

She explained her needs to Halldor, who told one of his men—one with a smattering of Gaelic—to go with her. Halldor himself kept watch over his son, while she went searching under guard of the Lochlannach.

She found it in the empty scriptorium, hanging from a peg near where the leather satchels would have been in peaceful times. The books, of course, had been carried to the tower, but in the confusion the *lés* was overlooked. She asked the Norseman who accompanied her if the tomes were already burned. No, came the halting answer. Halldor said not to.

On her way back she tried not to look at the round tower. At least the monks had died quickly, and earned the martyr's crown.

Dear God, if I save Halldor's son with Your help, perhaps he and his men will come to the True Faith. She hurried to the chapel.

Ranulf's breathing was slower, and he snored far back in his throat. "I will need better light," she told Halldor. He barked an order. A man bore the oil lamp nearer. Halldor himself held it close to Ranulf's head.

Brigit pulled back the boy's eyelids. The pupils were unequal, the left one large and black. She beckoned the lamp closer. The pupil did not shrink.

She pressed her lips together. Likely Ranulf would die, and she would soon follow him. "The skull is broken," she told Halldor, "and bone presses on his brain. There is much bleeding, you see. I will need to cut and tie."

"What will you require?"

"Light, and a strong man to hold it, who will not become ill." Even brave men often quailed at the sight of surgery. "And clean hot water, in two washed vessels. The other tools I have here." The *lés* held the sharp knife, the bone-saw, healing plants with which to pack the wound, the needles and thread—everything she needed save luck and the blessing of God.

Halldor gave directions in his alien tongue; his followers scurried to do his bidding. While she waited, Brigit prayed. "Our Father . . ." But when she closed her eyes, instead of God she saw only Conaill, her earthly father. Conaill, in his bluff way, had been fond of his baseborn daughter. Had he not sent her to be fostered by his aunt the abbess? In this time of war, if Conaill was yet alive, he might have been captured, might even be a slave himself. Brigit heard the men bring in the water.

There were two, both friends of Ranulf's, men who had also used her for their pleasure. They glowered, ashamed to do women's work, doubly

ashamed to serve their captive. *If I save Halldor's son, I'll no longer be molested by those churls*, Brigit thought. *And if I do not, I die.* She permitted herself a haughty gesture. The two brought the basins closer.

The water steamed in the cool air. First she should wash the wound. She needed a strip of clean cloth, and looked down at her own clothing. Pure it once had been, but today the rough homespun was ragged and bore streaks from the many times she'd been tumbled in the dirt.

Ranulf's blood pooled wider on the white altar cloth. Parts of the holy linen yet were clean. "I'll be needing a knife," she told Halldor. She saw how he tensed. Knives she had in the *lés*, but they were short, and she wished to keep them sharp. He did not trust her, then. Perhaps he thought she'd slay herself—or him? Ranulf's breathing grew slower. She had no time for games. "Would you have me heal your son? Give me your knife, then!" she snapped. Halldor reached to his waist, loosed the sheath, and handed his dagger over.

It was heavy in her hand, and the blade gleamed sharp. She studied it in the lamplight. Halldor was watching. *God forgive me*, she thought, and slit the altar cloth. Her strong hands ripped it the rest of the way.

She dipped the cloth into the steaming water and sponged Ranulf's head. When she dipped the cloth again the water reddened.

Best to work quickly. Brigit washed her hands and the surgical implements in the second basin,

and dried herself on the altar cloth. First cut a
flap of skin, leaving one edge attached, and ex-
pose the bone. With the small sharp knife she
scraped the flesh back. The splinters beneath
showed red and white; blood oozed between
them. She recalled how carefully she must pick
out each sliver. To do so would leave a gaping
hole in the skull—time to worry about that
later—but while it healed something must pro-
tect the naked brain. As she worked she spoke. "I
will be needing—" She thought. *Wood? No, it
should be pliable, and curved.* "A piece of leather,
the size of a man's palm. Tough leather, clean.
Have it boiled. Boil it until I call for it."

Again Halldor spoke; another of Ranulf's
friends went forth.

Blood oozed faster, then spurted. "More
light," Brigit said. Halldor held the lamp closer;
she glanced up and saw his face was pale. A
blood vessel there, and large. With a piece of
thread she tied it off. The pumping stopped. She
took a deep breath and dipped her gory hands
into the water. She'd never seen such a serious
wound. More often than not these patients soon
died. The bleeding had slowed to an ooze. With
needle and thread she stitched up the skin, using
not the running stitch for garments but a knotted, tied-off stitch that could later be removed—
if there was a later. Now that the bone was gone,
the skin could expand and leave room for bleeding. She sat back examining her handiwork.
Halldor yet held the light, though his arm shook.

She had done her best. Was it imagination, or

was Ranulf's breathing less labored? A final task remained. "Might I have the piece of leather now?" As she spoke she tore strips from the altar cloth. She swathed Ranulf's head with several layers of bandage; in the last layer she included the leather shield.

The last sunlight had faded. The chapel's single window looked out on night. *Dear God, bless my work.* Her knees buckled. Halldor set down the lamp and caught her.

Brigit and Halldor sat up with Ranulf, watching. In the uneasy flame-glow his face looked almost like a small boy's. The down on his cheeks was nigh-invisible, and his mouth lay relaxed. She looked at Halldor. Yes, behind Halldor's broken nose and thick, close-cropped beard, she saw a part of the same face. She thought of Ranulf's cruelty and shivered. His father had not touched her—not at the time of her capture, nor later, though she rode in his longship.

She rose and drew nearer her patient. His breathing had quickened, and his skin was flushed. The burning! So often did it follow surgery. At his wrist, the pulse too was fast.

Outside the door it was not far to the riverbank, but Halldor's eyes forbade her to leave. She found a vessel of holy water and tore a strip from her dress. No need here for cleanliness, and what modesty was left her? She sponged Ranulf's face and wrists, and settled back to wait.

Though Halldor had brought in his bedroll, neither of them lay down that night. Brigit, leaned against the wall, her knees drawn up to her chin, dozed from time to time. Her dreams were jumbled: God the Father, Conaill, and Halldor wore the same countenance.

When the first rays of morning crept through the chapel door, Ranulf moved, but only his left side. As the sun climbed higher he opened his eyes and tried to mumble a few words. His tongue was thick, and he could not be understood, even by his father. Brigit stopped Halldor from giving him mead. Instead she held a clean water-soaked rag to his lips.

When his eyes focussed enough that he could recognize her, he turned his head aside, but then he saw Halldor and lay quiet. "He needs water," Brigit said. "He will choke, lying flat. If you can raise his head and shoulders—" Halldor complied. Brigit pressed a water-bottle to Ranulf's mouth.

Helpless, he soiled himself, and she cared for him as if he were an infant. She'd helped swaddle her baby brother, after all, when her mother died in childbed. And she smiled. This man had beaten and humiliated her. Who was now the weak one?

She gathered the rags and garments to wash them, and looked to Halldor for permission. He nodded. "My son lives," he said. "You are safe, and I will so instruct my men." His hands shook. Purple marks underscored his eyes.

III

When Halldor trod forth into morning, he found the vikings well encamped, some in the tiny huts which had housed the monks, some in tents nearby. Cookfires burned, lookouts stood posted, men who were not otherwise busy sat cleaning and sharpening their gear, save for those with naught better to do than loaf or toss knucklebones or, elsewhere on the island, romp through a wild game of stickball. Egil and Sigurd had been hard at work, setting things to rights. Along with everything else, Halldor's own sea chest had been brought into the chapel and his sleeping bag unrolled on the floor. There he would stay, beside Ranulf his son.

The day was clear. A few white clouds were
adrift on mild breezes. Sunbeams from the east
brightened them, broke in sparkles on the river,
turned woodland crowns along its banks green-
gold. The shouts of the ball players rang merrily,
the smoke gave a bite to each lungful he drew, a
flight of crows passed by with homely voices. All
that he marked might bode well.

Egil drew nigh. "How goes it?" he asked softly.
He and Halldor had been friends a long while.

"There's hope for him."

"Wonderful! Seeing that wound, I'd never
have awaited—"

"No, nor I. They've knowledge we don't, the
Westmen." Halldor stared outward, gathering
words. "Their books here shall not be harmed.
Nor shall the Irishwoman. Nor shall anyone lay
hand on her against her will. Who does those
things will answer heavily to me. Pass that word
among the crews."

"Even if Ranulf dies?"

Halldor nodded. "I did wrong to threaten her
with death should that happen. I was over-
wrought. Whatever his weird is, how could she
stay it? But she's striven to save him who made
booty of her. That was well done."

For an eyeblink it was as if she stood before
him as at first, when Ranulf dragged her back to
the blazing convent after he and a half dozen
more had tupped her out in the field. Tall, slender, skin fair and freckled above strong bones,
hair close-cropped in nunnish wise but shining

otter-brown, she kept her shoulders straight in the muddied habit; and her eyes held the color and cold of a midwinter dusk. Later, on shipboard, that gray had softened the barest bit as he felt a little kindliness—Ranulf had just finished with her in the forepeak—and asked whence she came. Maybe it was because he knew her tongue, making her more than a dumb beast. She'd told him she was the leman-child of a chieftain. That must be the one to the north, somewhat inland. The raiders had not attacked his holdings, being too eager to get on to the Shannon. . . .

Egil shrugged. "As you wish. Better help make it known yourself, that she's under your ward. Meanwhile, what should we be doing?" With no way to foretell what would befall, the skippers had not deemed it worthwhile to lay out much of a plan.

The weariness slipped from Halldor. He'd often enough gone sleepless at sea; now he could stop grieving over his son, at least for a short span, and get on with tasks that needed him. "What would you say?" he asked. "I've not been thinking about it as I should."

"Well, we'd better get the Papas buried before they begin to stink, and other such chores, but none of that will take long. Already the men grow restless. Best we send a crew to scout the mainland today; but let them come back early with something to offer the gods. Else no few among our bold warriors will fear ghosts this night. Tomorrow we should start reaving in earnest."

None of Egil's words surprised Halldor, but that was good in itself. "You've a shrewd head on you, old fellow," he said. A tingling went through him. "I'll lead the first search, and the sacrifice afterward."

Though he himself feared no dead monks, nevertheless—*For Ranulf and his mending. For my house. What else brought me here but the need of my house?*

He came back near sundown and hastened to the chapel. "How is he?"

"Resting," Brigit answered, and showed him. Ranulf slept quietly on the altar, beneath an image of White Christ nailed to the cross. She had gotten him into a monastic robe, which was a loose garment, and rolled another up to be a pillow and spread a third across him for a blanket. He saw that she'd laid a few more down—as far from his sleeping bag as might be—for her own bed. He wondered how that might feel, to lie among the clothes of her slain landsmen.

His thought went away in a rush of gladness. Ranulf lived, Ranulf lived! At once he remembered that he must give Thor what he had promised, and soon. "Keep watch—" he began.

"I'd not be leaving here, save to empty yon pot," she told him coolly. "Too many barbarians about." That was bold of her, as worn and hollow-eyed and alone as she was.

"If any harms you, he dies, and they know it,"

Halldor blurted. In haste: "But do stand by my boy. We . . . this evening we hold a meal you'd not partake of. I'll have some flatbread and stockfish brought you."

Her look sought the one on the cross. "I thank you," she whispered, not to the man.

Halldor brushed a hand across Ranulf's brow, turned, and left. Later he saw her watching from the door. Was she curious? If so, he liked that too.

During the day, while he and his followers ranged the nearby mainland, Egil and Sigurd had seen to making ready on Scattery. Below the round tower now rested a boulder they had dragged from somewhere else, to be an altar; there was even a sign chiseled into the stone, the Wheel of the sun and the thunder-wagon. On top lay Halldor's hammer from his ship, short-hafted, heavy-headed. Also to hand were a knife, a bowl, and a swatch of wands from the island trees. Before the altar stood tethered the horse he had found on a man-empty farm and brought back in *Sea Bear:* a shaggy brown pony, shivering and rolling its eyes in bewilderment. Nearby, fire crackled beneath a kettle where water had begun to seethe. The vikings were gathered in a half-ring, garbed in the best they could bring forth after all their faring and fighting. Above them the sky lofted wan blue, deeper in the east, greenish in the west where the sun had dropped below a murk of mainland trees. The river glimmered, a few gulls hovered creaking.

As he walked forward, it rushed through

Halldor: *O Lord of Storm, take what I will give, and give me back my son!* A part of him snickered at himself: *Why, you're praying just like a Christian. Bargain with the Mighty Ones; what else can a man do? At that, it may well be foredoomed that they cannot help.* But meanwhile he begged: *Thor of the Weather, we've always been friendly, you and I, not so? Now listen. I'm not too old to beget more sons, whether or not Unn can bear them. But I am old enough to be aware of how soon and easily I may die. How then shall my house abide? Help*

Ranulf live!

He reached the altar stone and raised his arms. A stillness fell, broken by naught save river-flow and gulls.

Here there could be no great feast such as was held when folk flocked to a halidom in Norway. He only led the men in saying what was right to the high gods. He stunned the horse with the hammer, then cut its throat. Egil and Sigurd caught the blood in the bowl. Halldor dipped the wands there and sprinkled altar and gathering. The carcass was butchered; ale went around as flesh cooked in the kettle. Merriment lifted, and boastful vows were made over the horns. Stars came forth, torches and lesser fires were kindled. When the meal was ready, Halldor signed it. Meat and broth went to everybody's trenchers and thus to their gullets. Bones cast on the coals sent up a rich smoke that bade the gods come share in this feast.

Hard drinking followed. The ships had borne casks of beer; the monks had had more, as well as a few jugs of wine. Sprawled about on the ground, men chattered, or told stories of old which were thought to be lucky, or listened to staves from those among them who had some skaldcraft. Halldor did not stint himself. He needed a time of ease.

Fires were guttering low, Thor's Wain stood canted among the stars, chill had seeped through clothes, when he said goodnight and made his way through gloom to the chapel.

IV

The stench of horseflesh turned Brigit's stomach: a pagan feast on forbidden meat. From the chapel door she'd viewed the sacrifice, flinched as Halldor cut the poor beast's throat—though he'd stunned it first, she must admit. She'd watched the Lochlannach feed until night thickened around their fires. Now laughter and drunken song strove against the stars. On the very island Saint Senan claimed for Christ! Brigit wished, briefly, that the ancient monster might return to scatter these vile revellers, but if it had been banished by holy Senan it must be a creature of darkness.

As to sacrilege, she, a woman, should not be here. The founding saint had never allowed women, not even nuns, on his island, and for centuries the monks had kept his rule. But she had not come by choice.

Ranulf yet lay on the altar: more sacrilege, a pagan bedded on the Mass-table. But there his father had put him. Mostly he slept. When dreams troubled him only his left side thrashed. His right half was dead. Beside him lay his sword, where the men had set it. Well might it be that he'd never lift it again. He woke from time to time and watched Brigit with haunted eyes. He was at the mercy of his former captive, and could neither speak nor defend himself. Doubtless he expected the same treatment he'd given earlier.

Brigit need fear him no longer. She treated him as she was bid to aid any helpless creature.

The air in the earth-floored chapel was cool and damp. It hinted of mold, and the ghost of incense lingered. Such smells did not mask sickroom odors. If indeed her person was safe she might venture forth tomorrow for supplies, might gather herbs, do a laundry. Perhaps God had heeded her pleas.

More guffaws rose around the fires, and she heard shouted comments in Norse. She flinched. She did not speak this language, and for days all save Halldor had treated her as a dumb beast.

Someone fumbled at the chapel door. It gaped to the night, and Halldor stepped inside, swaying. Flecks of dried horse's blood sprinkled his face and clothing. He strode forward . and grasped her wrist. Wood-smoke, beer, leather, and man-sweat choked her. She could not free herself. She was no weakling, she was tall for a woman, but her head barely reached his chin. She refused to meet his gaze, and stared instead at his gold mantle-brooch. It resembled one her father's uncle had worn. Halldor must have stolen it.

Halldor's breathing quickened. "My son sleeps?" Wordless, Brigit nodded. He put an arm about her waist. She stood rigid. "Well have you wrought, caring for him. Fear no more wanton misuse. I have told the crews that you are mine alone."

Brigit turned her face toward the altar. She'd thought herself delivered, the more fool she. A taste of vomit stung her gullet. "I am no man's woman," she choked forth, "but a promised bride of Christ." Halldor might kill her for that. She hoped so.

Instead he laughed. She heard, she smelled how drunk he was. "Your Christ is a poor bride-groom, if he will not defend you. A woman such as you wants a strong man." He released her waist and grasped both wrists in one huge hand. With the other hand he turned her head toward him. She shut her eyes; she'd no wish to see *that* expression.

"Look at me, woman." His fingers on her jaw bruised afresh the marks Ranulf and his men had left. There was no help for her. She would be overpowered. She regarded him, holding her face motionless.

The lines around Halldor's blue eyes told of years spent searching the distance. What strange lands and seas had they surveyed? He did not look cruel, only drink-fuddled and surprised. Womenfolk must not often resist him. Despite his broken nose he was handsome, in his rough way, blond and tanned and weathered. But he had Ranulf's coloring and jawline. She shuddered, recalling beatings, pain, and coarse laughter. A remnant of angry pride made her stand straight.

"You are too sightly for a nun's narrow bed." Halldor smiled. "I'll not hurt you. There's no joy in that. Take off your clothes." He released her wrists.

Brigit stood still. *If I flee, the night is full of sottish robbers and murderers. And if I resist, he is stronger by far than I, and may withdraw his protection. Dear Lord God, surely You understand.* Astonishingly steadily, she untied her cincture, kissed it, and set it down. Her outer garment, torn and muddy, followed it, as did her linen underdress. Convent-trained in neatness, she folded everything with care.

At last she stood naked and shivering. Her body gleamed pale in the lamplight: small high breasts, a flat stomach, slender limbs marred now by scrapes and dark bruises. Would that God had made her ugly! She clenched fists at sides.

Halldor's gaze held admiration. He nodded.

"Sightly indeed." With one rough finger he traced the marks on her thighs. "You've been ill-used; no wonder you fear me. Young men have much to learn."

Brigit remained still while Halldor flung off his clothes. Sturdy he stood, well-muscled, his chest, belly, and loins dusted with golden hair. Where not seared by sun and salt, his skin shone fair. He was not ashamed to be naked.

Brigit had seen unclad men before, as patients, and in the past few days had known far too much of Ranulf and his friends. But Halldor was no invalid or stripling. She shuddered and hugged her arms across her breasts.

"You must be chilled," Halldor said. "My bedroll is warmer than the dead monks' robes." He laid a palm on the small of her back and urged her to where his blankets were arranged. She suffered herself to be led.

Dear God, waken Ranulf, send a distraction, anything, please. She might have shouted down the wind. There was no answer. She sank onto the rough wool.

Halldor lowered himself beside her. His hands scraped her skin. "Fair you are indeed." She spoke no word, and willed her mind elsewhere. Much practice she'd had, since her capture, in ignoring pain of every kind. But Halldor's touch distracted her, tugged her from half-aroused childhood memories back to the present. *Why will he not use me and be finished? What more does he want?* Sore she was, painfully so, after days of abuse. When Halldor entered her she bit her lip lest she cry out from the hurt. Ranulf and his friends had mocked her distress. *In a few moments he will be done. I am strong enough to bear anything for a brief time.* Then, practically: *At least there are not six others waiting their turn.*

She held onto the pain, but it faded, and yet the man thrust into her. Nohow could she ignore the slow and deliberate ravishment. Pain had at least helped occupy her mind.

Forever lingered, but at last he stopped plunging and cried aloud. His fingers bit into her shoulders as his body shook. He was quiet a while, then rolled off and lay facing her. She kept her gaze fixed on the roof. He'd been heavy; good it was to breathe again.

Halldor sighed. Brigit felt him rise on an elbow and reach out a hand. He did not touch her. He stayed that way a time before he turned over and pulled the blankets to his shoulders.

Only after he began to snore did Brigit permit herself to cry. Tears, the first since her capture, coursed down her face. *I've no escape at all. He'll neither kill me nor leave me in peace. God Himself has forsaken me, no, God forgive me my sin of despair.*

Shivering, she crept from bed and donned her underdress, lest Halldor wake and find her naked. She stared at the altar where Ranulf slept beneath the crucifix. The martyred Christ was strange and far away. Yet after she sought her pallet, darkness quickly claimed her.

V

The vikings were off before dawn. They left none behind save the badly wounded, Ranulf and two others. The island was safe; no Irish troop could be close enough to reach it suddenly. Nonetheless, it wrenched at Halldor to leave his son helpless, under care of a woman who had been bitterly wronged. But what was to be, would be, and idleness hurt worse.

Rowing back and forth across the river, the Norsemen sacked several farmsteads. Their gain was not great, mostly food and livestock. They met nobody; everyone had fled, and the woods brooded almost scarily quiet around the fields, beneath looming white clouds. "They've gone upriver, I think," Halldor remarked to one of Ranulf's young friends, who grumbled at the poor pickings. "There's an abbey that way— that's a steading of Papas akin to what we've overrun, but bigger—which serves as a stronghold. Also, a chieftain's hall isn't far off from it."

"Why don't we strike yonder at once, before they can gather strength?" the youth asked.

"Because the folk will bring all their best goods in hope of shelter, if we give them time. As for fighting men, the chief hereabouts can raise fewer than you might think. He's at odds with a strong neighbor and so must keep watch on his eastern march. Remember, I spied my way

through these parts, this past winter." Halldor
drew breath. "Oh, yes, belike the Irish host will
outnumber us when we meet them, and man for
man they're as good. But very few wear mail,
and none have yet learned how to fight in a
well-knit array. We can scatter them. Then
abbey and hall are ours, with everything therein,
and we can freely scour the countryside."

"How long till this happens?"

Halldor shrugged. "A week or two, maybe.
We'll see how it goes. Meanwhile we'll pick these
nearby shores clean."

"Well enough for you," the other said sulkily.
"You've grabbed the one woman on the holm for
yourself alone."

Halldor gave him such a scowl, half raising a
hand, that he dropped his gaze and slouched off.

Having taken whatever was in easy reach, the
vikings returned toward evening. Halldor made
haste to the chapel. His heart knocked and a
fullness held his throat. Beyond the door, night
already lay in wait, barely held at bay by a pair
of lamps. Brigit rose from crouching near the
altar and backed away. Halldor sought his boy.
"Ranulf—" he breathed.

Half hidden by swaddlings that had lately
been changed, stiffened on the right side, the
face at least lived. Eyes gave back yellow
flamelets. The tongue was thick, the speech hard
to understand. "Father . . . I don't think . . .
now . . . I'll walk hell-road."

Halldor wondered if Ranulf would ever walk

again at all. "How do you feel?"

"Less bad. Less pain. She . . . tends me well. . . ."

Halldor peered through the gloom toward Brigit. In her drab gown she was a shadow among shadows. "Come here," he said. Step by step she neared until she halted—behind the altar, to keep it between them. She leaned forward, bracing herself.

"How goes it with him?" Halldor asked. "Tell me truth. Have no fear."

She straightened, then: "Oh, I have no fear of death, if that is what you mean." Her tone flattened. "His fate is in God's hands. However, I think you may hope. He's strong, and mends faster than I'd have expected."

"What else does he need?"

"God's mercy. Beyond that—" She sought words for a bit, before saying in a rush: "Well, this building is unsuited for a sickroom. He could too easily take a chill. Move him to a monk's cell, where a small fire may keep him warm. And the sanctuary would no longer be profaned." She reached to touch the crucifix. "I'll ask Him Above to take that kindly."

Halldor felt his lips crease upward. "You do right well by us, your foes, Brigit."

"Christ commands forgiveness of wrongs," she said harshly.

He regarded her a while before he murmured, "Can anything else be done for Ranulf?"

"Yes." Her answer came at once; she must

have been thinking about this. "It may happen
or not that he never again uses his right-side
limbs. But in either case, it would help to flex
and rub them often. Tomorrow I mean to begin
that, if you wish. Yours is to tell him why, first,
and say he must endure the pain and himself try
to move."

"Good!" burst from Halldor, almost gladly.
"If aught can be done—Let's see to shifting him
at once." He stood unspeaking for a time. "You,
though, lass, you're near to breaking."

She made no answer.

When his new bed had been readied, a fire lit
on the tiny open hearth, and he borne there,
Ranulf fell into a heavy, snoring slumber. One of
his comrades sat by, at Halldor's bidding, to let
his nurse get a rest. "Well, I see, skipper," the
young man said. "She's no good to him if she
keels over, is she? Or to anyone else." He cast her
a lickerish glance. Halldor knew she understood
no word, but her cheeks went whiter still. She
knotted her fists and turned her back.

"Come." He took her elbow. She flinched, but
they walked forth together.

Wood-smoke and a racket of men filled the air,
mingled with lowing and grunting, bleating and
cackling of creatures brought hither. A number
of the Norse were building pens and coops out of
wood lopped from the grove at the west end of
the island. Brigit watched this and breathed, as
if to herself: "Now the sea winds will blow cold

across the graves of the old monks, and the unhallowed pit where those lie that you killed. May God give warmth to their souls." Her gray eyes stared into distance.

Somehow uneasy, Halldor said, "Since we've been on the move throughout this day, we'll eat our big meal now—rather, when it's ready. I hope you're not starved."

She turned her face toward him, cheekbones sharp beneath the skin. "I'll be eating none of your food, I've decided."

Shocked, he remembered the custom they had in this land, of fasting against an oppressor. If she wasted away, who would care for his son? At once, as if of itself, the unshakability of a trader came over him, and he merely shrugged. "Would you like some fresh air, anyhow? You've seen nothing but sickroom."

With hope, he heard that a half sob answered. He beckoned slightly and paced south. She hung back, then followed. Side by side, an arm's length between, they went that way which led farthest from camp.

Westward the sun had sunk behind mainland trees. Above their darkling wall, clouds glowed gold. Elsewhere blueness lingered, and the river sheened. A breeze brought faint chill and smells of springtime growth. Rooks cawed in flight. The sod, green with new grass, studded with wildflowers, felt soft underfoot, as if helpless. Though the island was flat and small, walking soon made the man-racket dwindle till it was well-nigh lost.

That stillness weighed on Halldor. He must speak: "Brigit, who are you?"

"What?" she asked, startled out of wherever she had gone.

He brought his eyes toward her. Fair she was, he saw. Take off the haggardness, make her smile, and no man could wish for a handsomer woman. But he doubted she would ever smile at him. "I owe you thanks," he said awkwardly. "You see, Ranulf is my last son alive."

Staring straight ahead, she mocked in a dull voice, "I'd think you could beget more. Have you no wife at home?"

"Yes, but Unn seems to have grown barren, and besides—" He snapped his teeth together. Why should he bare himself to a thrall?

She was not a thrall. Enough whipping and hunger might turn her into one. He'd seen that happen, and did not want it for her.

He swallowed and began anew. "I owe you thanks. I pay my debts. What would you have of me?"

She halted. Slowly, starting to tremble, she confronted him, who had stopped likewise. Her whisper blazed: "My freedom."

He nodded. "If Ranulf lives, you'll go free. If he is no cripple, you'll have reward as well."

"That, that lies . . . with God . . . not me," she stammered.

"Call on your God, then." In quick slyness, Halldor added, "Of course, it'll be no use if you

let yourself die of hunger." He saw her will about
that melt away. In all else, however, she must
still be withstanding him. He rubbed fingers
across beard, thinking aloud. "Will it help if we
leave him alone in his kirk? I'd sooner raise my
tent anyhow, now that my boy is elsewhere. It
can hold a knockdown bedstead and it's well-
oiled, to shed your Irish rain."

She stiffened afresh. He walked on. She fell in
beside him. "You will understand, I have to
make sure you'll do your best for Ranulf," he
said. "If you fail and he dies, well, you'll not find
me an unkindly owner. But otherwise—let's be
honest. Even if a . . . a miracle, do you call it?
. . . even if he were healed overnight, it'd be no
boon to set you loose. You'd be prey. If you happened on a countryman of yours, he might help
you home, or he might not; either way, your
convent is no more. There'll be scant peace in
this land after we're gone. No, instead will be
outlaws, men driven wild by woe, attacks from
those of your own folk who're at loggerheads
with your lord.

"I can do better for you than that, Brigit."

She glared at him. "Can you indeed? You sav-
ages swoop down, make ruin, and are gone, till
we've built up again what it pleases you to plunder."

"I'm no viking of my own wish," he told her.
"I've traded in the Westlands for many years.
How else would I have learned your tongue?"

Her lips grew thin. "Why then are you playing

pirate?"

"Ill luck." Strange, he thought, that he gave
her the tale so readily. "My father was a well-off
yeoman in Thrandheim. That's a kingdom in the
land called Norway." Sharply before him rose
the great bright bay, where islands dreamed and
boats went dancing; the sturdy wooden houses
of Nidaros town, the life that brawled in its
lanes; the hills beyond, wildwoods, farms, home.

"I being his third son, no land would fall to
me," Halldor said. "Besides, I was restless. I
became a hunter and trapper, who early went on
ships bound north to Finnmark and Bjarmiland.
There we'd gather things like hides, walrus
tusks, fine pelts. Soon I was in a crew bearing
them overseas to these western countries. In
time I won enough wealth to buy my own acres,
raise my own garth, wed—and, yes, have two
ships in trade, not these lean dragons but good
big-bellied *knarrs*—"

He mustered calm. "Well, my father took sick
and was a long while a-dying. My oldest brother
Thorstein is a hothead, often in viking, unwise as
a farmer. My second brother . . . set off for Russia, and the ship was never seen again. That was
a heavy loss, for he bore a rich cargo to barter,
mostly bought with borrowed money. Thorstein
quarreled with a neighbor, it came to blows,
men were slain or badly hurt. The Thing—the
folkmoot—deemed Thorstein at fault. He must
pay more than he had in weregilds, or be outlaw.
Of course, I helped him pay. But I'd overreached

myself, too. Big dowries for both my daughters to get them well wedded, and money in ships or out in loans I could not recall at once. . . . The upshot was, if I would save my homestead, I must win wealth fast. So I swapped one freighter for the warcraft you've seen and joined a viking fleet readying for Ireland.

"That was year before last. I've enough now, or ought to after I'm through here, that I can go back. Thereafter I'll be what I erstwhile was. This faring cost me my elder son, and maybe it will cost me Ranulf too. If he dies, what have I saved my home for?"

He had said too much, and broke off. They reached the southern tip of land. Between them and the bank flowed two miles of river. It went murmurous, aglow as sunset climbed and strengthened. The air was growing damp.

Brigit crossed herself and muttered a prayer. Then she challenged him: "If robbery pays better, why would you rather be a chapman?"

Astonished, he answered, "Why? Well, raiding pays better for the few, not the many. Also, well, I take no pleasure in harming folk who never harmed me. I'd rather fare about, from the reindeer herders in Finnmark to the lofty halls in York and London—and, yes, even your abbeys—I like talking with strangers, learning about them. A foeman can't."

"How can you, a pagan, deal with men of faith?" Her tone was sharp-edged.

"Oh, I got me prime-signed long ago."

She gave him a puzzled look. "Prime-signed, yet not baptized?"

"No. I'll not forsake Thor of the Weather. We get along well, Redbeard and I."

She flared. "Proud must that demon be of you!" Her voice dropped. "Still, I'll be praying that your son be healed."

Halldor shrugged. "Yes, so you can go free. That's between you and your own god." His mouth crinkled. "Don't forget to eat, though."

Suddenly: "But are you maybe a witch, Brigit? I asked you about yourself, and instead spun you my yarn. Now do tell me who you are, that I may think what's the best bargain I can offer you."

Calming, she nodded—sundown turned her curls to molten bronze—and gazed across the water to a woodland drenched with amber light. After a silence she spoke, softly and slowly:

"My life has been less varied than yours. My father is Conaill MacNiall, lord over the land where my convent stood. Before you burned it. My mother was his slave, but he was good to us both. She died later, birthing my brother, when I was six years old. Next year I was of an age to be fostered, so Father sent me to his aunt the abbess."

"Why?" Halldor wondered. "In Norway, well-born children often go as fosterlings into households more lowly, but that's to teach them skills, and to bind both families closer. What gain here?"

"Oh, I was slave-born. He gave me to the Church as payment for his sins."

Brigit stood quiet. A salmon leaped in the river. All at once she blurted: "Besides, Father's wife could never abide my mother. Not that she minded him bedding her, but you see, Mother was of the Old Way—She was christened, of course, but she'd make offerings to the Sídhe, and it was Samhain and Bealtaine, not All Souls' and Lady Day, that she kept—" A pause, a gulp. "Father let her. I fear he's not the Christian he might be, and I pray for his soul, and for poor Mother's. She was a simple girl from the bogs. There the Old Way still goes luring among the mists—" A finger flickered through the sign of the cross, twice, thrice. "Holy Mother Mary, blessed Saint Brigit my namesake, I thank you that I was saved."

"Then you've liked being a . . . a nun?" Halldor asked low.

"*Yes!*" Brigit nearly hissed it, while she stared into distance like a blind woman. "After I watched Mother serve Father and his wife at table—then sit at the far end of the hall, away from fire and honor—she who loved him—I watched her die screaming in childbed. Oh, tended she was by that other woman, but coldly, coldly. Father himself could not come to her; that wouldn't beseem a man. Then why should any woman ever wish to serve a man?"

"But man and woman can be shipmates through life—" Halldor quit his clumsy search for words. What he had wanted to speak of was such an uncommon thing anyhow. Could he honestly say that he and Unn had ever quite known it? In a way, but—And Brigit, thus far, was merely prey.

He needed to hearten her, for Ranulf's sake. At

the back of his head, there passed through him
that that could be for his own sake too. "You're a
spirited lass," he said. "Did you really find joy in
poverty, obedience, and singing songs to your
god?"

She swung to face him. Her gaze was no longer
blank, but matched her words. "Do you suppose,
you benighted heathen, that we did naught but
pray? Why, prayer was our rest, our joy. We were
never idle—work—gardening, cooking, cleaning, brewing, tending the animals, housing
wayfarers, caring for the poor, the sick, the
hurt—How do you think I learned leechcraft?
Chopping helpless people up, like you? No, I
went about the whole parish, fearless, my person
sacred, the honored guest of lord and crofter
alike. For that lord or his merchant friend, I'd
write a letter, or read one that came to him.
Home again, I'd study Scripture, the lives of the
saints, the wisdom of the ancients—we had
Virgil—but what would Virgil mean to you, you
illiterate pagan? And as the abbess grew old and
weak, I her niece helped her more and more to
govern our sisterhood—"

He thought fleetingly that the convent, hum-
bler than this monastery had been, was about as
much as his wife had to steer, or less. On the
other hand, at home there were no dealings with
priests, bishops, far-off Romaborg, the weight of
hundreds upon hundreds of years. . . .

"Then you came, you murderers, bandits,
wolves!" Brigit screamed. "You scattered

us—all but me, and would God I'd gotten away
to die in the wildwood!—you looted, you burned,
you ruined it all—Oh, Hell will have you!" She
lifted crooked fingers to the sky. "Holy Senan,
you drove the sea beast from this island." Her
teeth gleamed in a mouth stretched wide. "Call
it back against *these* beasts!"

She had drawn the reins too tight upon herself, Halldor saw. They had snapped. He could
hardly blame her. A Norsewoman with her kind
of heart would have taken a gruesome revenge
and died, like Brynhild and Gudrun—or, if
naught else could be, turned a knife on
herself—but Brigit was Christian and debarred
from that freeing. Still, he couldn't let her run
mad. Ranulf needed her.

He slapped her cheeks, right, left, right, left.
The blows cracked aloud. Her head rocked back
and forth. Her screeches came to a halt and she
stared at him out of eyes gone huge.

"That will do," he said. "We can talk more,
later. But first let's go back."

Dumbly, she stumbled after him. Sunset
began to fade.

—At camp, she soon came out of her shock, as
he had awaited. She even found some orders to
pass, through him, to three of Ranulf's friends,
who were to care for the wounded youth overnight. "Should anything untoward happen,"
Halldor told them, "you can call her from my
tent."

One fellow leered. "As for what else she may

need," he asked, "can I help out . . . again?"

Halldor flushed. "No. She's earned that much respect." None of them dared further mirth, at least until he was gone.

—Stretched across two pairs of poles whose ends were carved into ravens' heads, and a shaft between them, the tent was high enough at the peak for a man to stand upright. It held a warm, strong smell of grease, leather, fire. A lamp cast flickery light and restless shadows. Pegged together, a bedframe was covered with bearskins; they were bulkier than straw tick and wool blanket, but stayed fresher when a man fared overseas.

Halldor looked long upon Brigit. She gave it back to him.

"If you heal Ranulf," he said at last, "shall I take you home to your father, and help him make such alliances among the Norse that he need not fear them?"

"That would be well," she mumbled.

How strong and fair she stood, he thought; and he offered in a suddenness that surprised him: "Any child you bear, I'll provide for if no one else does."

She did not smile at his words, but flinched. "You would not leave me alone . . . until I am free?"

"No," he said, for he could say nothing else. "You are too fair. But I'll try to be kind, Brigit."

She turned her face away, which hurt. Nevertheless he went to her.

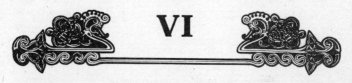

VI

Twilight greyed the Shannon. The crews would soon return. Brigit sat in Ranulf's doorway, savoring her last moments of solitude. Across the fields, smoke rose from the ruins of another home. Days, now, they'd harried the land, and few folk were left. Those who tried to resist were slaughtered. *Damn the raiders to the blackest pits.* Far up the river she saw longships. She went inside.

Despite her best efforts, the hut was damp and chill, and the sickroom stench fought the sweetness of straw and herbs. Ranulf lay quiet, on clean bedding. His eyes were blank.

"They are coming now," Brigit said, in the few Norse words she'd learned. On the shore hulls scraped over pebbles, hearty voices laughed and jested. Ranulf turned his head away. "War and plunder are not everything," said Brigit. He did not answer.

As soon as *Sea Bear* landed, Halldor hastened to the hut and stood looking down at his son. The firelight gilded the youth's hair and his few wisps of beard. In that light, with his eyes closed, he seemed a child. Halldor's garments reeked of smoke, and his boots were foul. He stood silent a moment. "He mends?"

Brigit nodded. *His body, anyhow.* "Today he moved the fingers of his right hand. Strength returns."

Halldor's shoulders slumped. She saw how tense and weary he was. "You have done well, woman." He reached into his pouch and drew forth an object. It gleamed. "Then have a leech-gift of me."

She stretched out her hand before she saw what it was. A gold collar! She dropped it as if burnt. "You have robbed a faerie-mound!" She scrubbed her hand on her skirt. "That is gold of the Old Ones, the Sídhe, it bears a curse!"

"It was only a stone-heaped grave," said Halldor, "and no ghost rose against us. We have the same in our country, though I'd not trouble my kinsmen's grave-goods. You have worked well."

Brigit backed away. "No! This is cursed by the ancient gods—I dare not touch it—death and madness!"

He shrugged. "Strange, you Christians. If your god is all-powerful, why fear the ancients?" He picked up the collar and returned it to his pouch. "I'd not willingly distress you. My wife Unn will wear it with pride."

Brigit fought horror long enough to think, *He wished to please me.* She raised her head. "If you'd truly reward me, Halldor—"

He smiled. "Set you free? I've agreed to that, when my son no longer needs your care. And if you'd plead again that I not touch you, remember I am a man."

"No, it is a smaller boon I ask." Brigit paused. "The monks here kept books, many more than did my convent." *Before you and your bandits sacked it.* She bit back the words. "Ranulf is less ill now, and can be left for longer periods. Might I have leave to study the volumes in my free time? One of your men said they survive by your order."

Halldor nodded. "You have leave, if Ranulf is tended."

Brigit bowed her head and murmured thanks. *The illiterate pagan!* But at least he'd spared the books.

Her hand that had touched the collar felt filthy. She slipped from the hut.

Chill wind swept the island, bearing scents of river and early spring. A few stars gleamed through the cloud-streaked sky, but most of Heaven's lamps were left unlit. Unseen in the gloom, the river chuckled.

Brigit sought Saint Senan's holy well. The vikings did not know of it, and it was the one place on the island left undefiled. Shallow, it trickled from the moss to pool in a tiny rock-lined basin. Brigit felt as if she had clasped something dead, though many the corpse she had washed and laid out with never a qualm.

She knelt and sank both hands into the water. Whispers went on the night wind, and she shivered. *Saint Senan, save me from those who ride in the dark! And Brigit, my namesake, deliver me from bondage.* But the night would not be still.

The way back to camp was long, and gloom rustled about her. Halldor's tent-lamp made a warm yellow beacon. She crept inside. He did not ask where she had been.

After he used her she did not lie staring into blindness, but fell instead into troubled dreams. In another, brighter world, a tall woman called her "my child, my namesake." But this woman was garbed in a silken gown and green mantle, and her eyes were milk-white. She wore no cross, and her golden hair blew unbound. "I am Brigit, and I have heard your plea." She reached out a hand and mortal Brigit woke, chilled with sweat. She lay listening to Halldor's steady breath and the tap of rain on the tight-stretched tent skins. Her right hand was chill. That was no saint, she knew. When she called, who had answered?

Dawn came grey and wet. Wind tossed waves against the stony beach. The season might have been midwinter.

"We'll not fare out today," Halldor said, surveying the sky. "I do not like yon clouds." He pointed to where murk roiled in the west. "Work enough have we done of late; a man must also rest." He let the tent-flap drop, and smiled.

Brigit dressed quickly and went to check on
Ranulf. She must find refuge—

He looked pale in the dim light. The hut was
colder than usual. Brigit built up the fire, fed and
bathed him, and changed the bedding. The
morning exercises were hurried. She was eager
to reach the scriptorium.

Grudging the time, she gnawed a dry crust of
bread. She refused to eat with the vikings, and
though Halldor made food available, she took as
little as she could and yet live. As she washed it

down with ale, Halldor appeared in the doorway.

"Your son should be all right for a while," she
said. "Perhaps he'd like to spend some time with
you. His exercises are finished. If you've no need
of me," *Please God he has none!* "I'll be with the
books."

Halldor nodded. His eyes were on his son.
Ranulf struggled to rise, but fell back. Brigit saw
Halldor frown, as if thinking, before she escaped
outdoors.

The rain fell heavier now. She hoped the
storage-hut was tight. Books were so easily
spoiled. She approached the small wattle-and-
daub building and pushed open the wicker door
to darkness.

Two bronze lamps hung on chains, and she
found the flask of oil, but she must go back for
fire. So anxious had she been to get away—no,
she would not return to Ranulf's hut. Halldor
was there. She went instead to the main
cooking-fire in the center of camp. Several crew
members sat idle under a nearby lean-to. No one
addressed her as she took a brand, but one of
Ranulf's friends muttered something, and was
answered by low laughter.

Her cheeks flamed. She held her head high as
she walked away.

After she adjusted the smoky wicks, light
showed that the earthen floor was dry and the
leather satchels on their pegs hung oiled and

mildew-free. All was as it should be, left by careful hands. Then she realized: the monks had of
course taken the volumes to the tower for
safekeeping; how came they then back here? She
shivered, seeing ghostly hands scrabble from
shallow graves, dead feet creep up bloodstained
ladders to gather their beloved books. Almost
she fled the place. *In the night, in the mist, after
the slaughter, while I saved a pagan life*—But then
she recalled that Halldor had given orders. She
reached toward the satchels. They swung heavy
with the weight of manuscripts.

Halldor must have pillaged many scriptoria, she
raged, *else he'd not know how they were kept*. She
lifted a bag from its peg.

The leather was embossed. She stroked the
interlaced design. Finer by far than those her
convent owned—*had owned.* Six books this
monastery had! She opened the one she held. A
Gospel book, two volumes, Luke and John. She
put it back. And next to it, yes, Matthew and
Mark. A copy of the Psalms, as well; a life of Saint
Brendan the Navigator, who'd sailed down this
very River Shannon to fare across the sea; and
the Life and Rule of Saint Senan. She looked at
this last in dismay. Senan had scant use for
women, she knew. What did he think of one in his
very monastery? Her fingers strayed toward the
final satchel. This leather clasp was stiffer than
the others, less-used. She drew forth a thin volume, sparsely-illuminated. She squinted at the
cramped writing. Hippocrates?

The Physician! *And for a pagan you'll leave the Lord's own words unread?* Her inner voice sounded like the old abbess'. *Enough of that; no fault of his he lived before Christ and had no chance to hear the Truth. Mayhap he became a saint when Our Lord harrowed Hell. He was a good man.*

She moved closer to the hanging lamp, taking care that no oil might drip onto the page. She whispered thanks that this was a Latin translation, for she read little Greek.

She jumped when the door creaked. Halldor bowed his head to clear the doorway. "Is all as it should be here?"

"The books are safe." Brigit clutched the volume. It had no gold leaf, few pictures, and no jeweled cover. Surely he'd not seize it?

"The men misliked my orders," Halldor said, "but I've long known that a book may be a treasure. What is it you have there?" He reached out. Brigit surrendered the tome; at least his hands were clean.

"A collection of writings by Hippocrates. He was a Greek physician who lived long before Christ."

"And his words wandered past his lifetime, far from his own land?" Halldor looked thoughtful. "I have never fared to Greece, but I've drunk with some who did. Bright sun, tiny islands in a dreaming sea—well, the world is wide. No man can see it all." He looked down at the page. "Yet those marks are his words, long after he lies cold." He smiled and handed back the volume. "So what does this great man say, that has been preserved so long?"

Brigit ruffled through the leaves. "Here is one that may pertain to how I treated your son: *Extreme remedies are very appropriate for extreme diseases.* Though I think Hippocrates would not have done as I did. His way was more with herbs. I've seen herbs fail too often." She looked up at Halldor, his brown face weather-scored, his

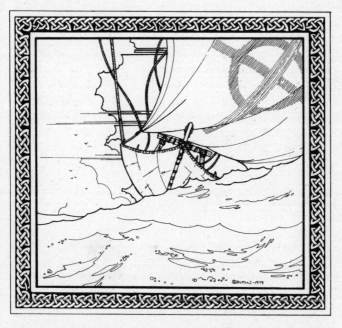

beard and hair showing first streaks of grey, and said, slyly, "Another here: *Old people have fewer diseases than the young, but their diseases never leave them.*"

Halldor flexed his fingers. His mouth twisted. "Right," he said. "No fevers burn me, nor the wasting cough, but year by year these hands creak more when they wrestle cold lines, or grasp the tiller in an icy fog." He closed one eye. "Ah, the stiffness of old age!"

Brigit blushed and gripped the book.

Halldor smiled. "Well, what else have you here?" He gestured to the other satchels.

Brigit spoke in haste. "Gospels, and a life of Saint Brendan the Navigator, and also of Saint Senan, who founded this monastery and banished a monster from this very island."

Halldor chuckled. "Banished a monster? Well for us that he did!"

Would it might return and drive you hence.

"This Brendan—I've heard he was a sailor too."

"Brendan sailed west with a crew of monks in search of Tir na n'Óg."

"Did he find it? Got he much plunder?"

"He went, you heathen, to bring the Word of God!" Brigit half-rose, but sank back to her stool. After that outburst he'd burn the books. . . .

He showed no sign of anger. "How dull, to fare with monks. Fish, bitter beer, and prayer. Did he find the land he sought?"

"Yes, he did," snapped Brigit, "and brought back fruit and gems from the sinless folk who lived there."

"Ah." Halldor's gaze was far away. "He found land to the West." Again he flexed his fingers, and his smile was bitter. "Not for me to go there. But my son? . . . Best you go see to him."

Wordless, Brigit snuffed the lamps and latched the scriptorium door.

In his invalid's hut, Ranulf stared at the

thatched roof. He spoke to Halldor, who translated: "He hates being lifted like an infant that he might take food and drink."

"He must be improving indeed, if complaints are any sign," said Brigit. "But he cannot sit unsupported, and when I prop him up he falls to the right. He's been learning to eat with his left hand." As she spoke she checked the bedding. It must be changed again, and in this weather the blankets would never dry. Halldor stood silent for a time, then left the hut. In a while she heard sawing and hammering.

She laundered the bedding on the shore and headed through twilight back to the scriptorium. Perhaps she could snatch some time by herself. Perhaps if she stayed late, Halldor would be asleep.

This time, in penance, she took down a Gospel-book. She'd been lax in her devotions. Devotions indeed! And when had she time? She bent over the scripture, hoping to lose herself in the sacred words.

She'd read several chapters of John when a gust of chill air ruffled the pages and blew out the lamps. Brigit looked up. A figure blocked the door. She flinched, then from the shoulders and height recognized Halldor.

"The hour grows late, and the storm will clear by dawn," he told her. "We'd best to bed."

Wordless, she returned the book to its satchel and followed him.

Standing in the yellow lamplight inside the

snug skin tent, Brigit tried to delay. "You told
me you'd sailed to northern waters, and seen
things such as those Brendan described?"

Halldor sat on the bed and removed his boots.
"Indeed I have. Look at this leather." He held
forth one boot for her inspection. Once more his
look went afar. "I might fare there again some
day. It was north that I first sailed, in my trading
days." He grinned suddenly. "Their land is cold
yonder, but not their women! Ah, that autumn
reindeer-gathering when I guested among the
Samek!"

Brigit cringed. Should she be surprised that
Halldor had known many women, and remembered them with joy? Moreover, he had a wife
and legitimate children.

Halldor set down his boots and began to re-
move his clothing. "Those were good times. But
we are here and now." Brigit sat beside him.
Would he mention her to some future con-
cubine? Perhaps by then she would be dead. She
began to shiver. Halldor held her close, and she
did not pull away from his warmth.

Halldor had predicted right: dawn came clear
and brilliant. Brigit woke alone. The crews were
already raiding, she knew, gathering the last
goodness from the land. She rolled over on the
bearskins and sneezed. The reflex made her gag.
She sat up and felt dizzy. Weak from scanty
meals, no doubt; but why did the thought of food
repel her?

She'd fallen asleep naked. Now she looked
down at her body, white against the furs. Blue
veins traced across her swollen breasts—she had
always been slight-figured. *It cannot be.* But her
time was days overdue. She'd counted on the
bleeding to keep Halldor away, and it had not
come. *Ah, it's only worried I am, for no cause.*
She swung her legs from beneath the covers and
reached for her garments. Her throat closed and
her mouth watered. She took deep breaths.
There. That was better. She ventured a weak

smile. Did legend not have it that Saint Senan struck barren any woman who trod his island?

She wanted to snuggle down amid the furs and sleep, but she must get on with the day. She pulled her shift over her head.

Flat and helpless, Ranulf just the same smiled at her. He spoke with care, trying Gaelic. "My father made a gift." He gestured to one of his attendants and spat a few Norse words. The man propped him up and raised a sheepskin-covered board behind his back. Brigit marveled at the construction: the hinges were leather, the backboard formed a triangle with the braces which locked into each other, and the right side had a padded shelf for support. She bent closer. The heathen sign of the Hammer was graven into the wood.

"My father," Ranulf said with pride, "built this yesterday." He leaned back at an angle and did not fall.

So that is how he spent his rainy day. She brought Ranulf his food. He had a better appetite than she'd seen before.

After he was settled, Brigit left the hut. She'd meant to seek the scriptorium, but took, instead, the left-hand path toward the sacred well.

She felt better by far than when she'd first risen. The grass sprang vivid green beneath her feet. By daylight the pool was in no wise dark or foreboding. It shimmered back at the sky, and was so shallow she could touch bottom without wetting her elbow. The moss smelled rich, and the water trilled into the basin.

She sipped water and rinsed her face. "Holy Brigit, my namesake, help me. I meant to live and die a virgin. Let me not bear a child." She closed her eyes to pray, but saw instead:

Lamplit gloom. A woman tossing on bloodstained straw. Her hair flew damp and tangled, and her face shone grey. She bit her lip to keep from screaming.

Burnt herbs sharpened the air. A shadow figure raised the woman's head and gave a drink, but she gagged. Her breath came shrill and rapid.

The shadow figure spoke. "The birthing's gone wrong. Conaill will mourn his favorite slave. Naught can be done that I know of. A pity; she served us well."

Brigit wept. Well had she chosen her life, and what had it availed? *Did I choose from fear, or for love of God?*

"There's little left for taking in these parts," Halldor remarked. Dark it was already; they'd been gone all day. He set down his eating-bowl.

"A pity, that you've stolen it so fast," she said. "And driven the folk from their homes as well, so great your diligence!" A shadow fell across where she sat on the bed.

Halldor had risen to stand above her. He smelled of fire. "If your folk lack strength to defend themselves, it's their fate."

She wondered, briefly, if he would strike her. She did not care. But he stepped back.

"You know all this. Yet tonight—I've no wish to strike you unless I must. What troubles you?"

If I do not tell him it may go away. "I've no way to get shriven, no way to attend Mass. The chapel here is desecrated, the monks and priests lie dead, and you keep me on this island as your slave!" She glared at him. "Well do I tend your son, though you know I could have done him harm, but for my own needs you care not at all!"

Halldor frowned. "What would you have me do?"

"Well you know what I'd have you do. Leave me in peace!" She could not let him see her cry.

He looked her full in the face. "As you wish. We sail at dawn, to be away several days. You will stay with Ranulf and two of the wounded." She retreated to the corner. He sat on the bed and drew off his boots, then looked at her in surprise. "You need not sleep on the floor. I've said I would not touch you tonight."

She hesitated, then crept in beside him when he slept.

Dawn-birds screeched above the raucous shouts as men hauled their ships to deeper water. Brigit curled into the furs. They'd roust her forth soon, that Halldor might take his tent.

But when she woke again all was quiet. Halldor had left not only his son, but his campsite in her care. She rose, fighting nausea,

and donned her outer clothing.

Wind whipped across the barren isle. Where dragonships had dotted the bay, the water gleamed empty. Where tents had sprawled on the green, only pegmarks and bits of offal remained. The great cooking fire was a smoking charcoal pit. Brigit turned and, for the first time, dared to look at the round tower.

It stood high as ever. They'd lit no fire, then, to make of it a chimney. Of course not, the books were safe. But she'd heard the screams of mur-

dered monks. Now their unblest graves were lapped by river tides.

She walked through morning mist to the hut where Ranulf lay, near his two attendants. From their fuddled expressions they'd drunk deep the night before.

She was alone now with the three of them. Ranulf would be no problem, but the other two were of his band. They and he had tumbled her in the dirt countless times. While she had little Norse, they had less Gaelic.

She'd learned a few words, though. She
stepped inside the hut and pointed to a bucket.
"Water," she said, "and firewood." One of the
men glowered but limped off to do her bidding.
The other sat sullen in a corner. *So they fear
Halldor.* She felt brief gratitude, and began
Ranulf's exercises. Perhaps, with her few words,
she could tell him more of Christ.

Days of waiting passed, and still Brigit's time
did not come. Ever more the morning mist sick-
ened her. She spent hours talking with Ranulf,
trying to instruct him in the Faith. When not
with him she stayed in the scriptorium, save
when she crept late at night to Halldor's empty
tent.

Ranulf's two friends remained sulky, but
caused no trouble. He could raise his right arm
now, move the toes on his right leg, and manage
the slant-board by himself. *Halldor made it for
his son*, Brigit thought, and ran her hand across
the Hammer. *Would Conaill had carved even a
doll for me.*

The bedding stank, and must be washed. Once
on her way to the riverbank she looked at the
abandoned chapel. She'd not gone there since
Ranulf was moved. She set the soiled cloths into
the river, weighted them with rocks, and
stepped away from the shore.

The chapel was dank. Mushrooms sprouted on
the untrod floor. Still the crucifix, black wood

bearing the White Christ, glimmered above the altar. Brigit knelt, then picked it up and carried it forth. Ranulf made no comment as she set it above his bed. His friends, when they came in, looked afraid.

Daily Brigit worried more. Perhaps the legend granted sterility to Saint Senan's tomb only, not his island? Although she slept there, or rather shivered all one rainy night, she had no sign. Too fretful to be still, she wandered the island. The round tower held the memory of blood. She went instead to the sacred well.

Daily as she fed or cleaned Ranulf, or moved his limbs, she would say, "I do this in the name of Christ," and gesture at the crucifix. She taught him also, as part of his exercises, to make the Sign of the Cross.

When he cried out with pain she put the cross into his hands and pointed at the Sacred Wounds. "See, then, what Christ did for you?"

"I've seen wounded men," said Ranulf. He handed the crucifix back.

Perhaps that was a beginning. Yet that same night, as Brigit lay in Halldor's bed, in Halldor's tent, she could not sleep. Almost she could imagine Halldor himself beside her—and almost she wished it were so. She rose and knelt until her knees ached and she trembled, then lay on the hard ground to sleep.

Next morning rain slashed the island and the river tossed grey-and-white waves. *Bad weather for travel*, Brigit thought. Halldor was due home today—but would he dare the Shannon in the storm? And why should she care for one who'd been out raiding her own land?

Still, during the day she stepped to the door of the hut or the scriptorium and looked upriver into greyness, until at last she saw the prow of the *Sea Bear*. Then she stepped indoors, ignoring the triumphant shouts as the men returned.

"Your father comes," she told Ranulf. "I will go to the chapel."

VII

When the keel of his ship touched ground, Halldor sprang from the steering oar, forward across the benches, and overboard at the bow. His crew could draw her up and make her fast. They understood his need. Water squelched chill in his shoes as he ran toward the monastery. Rain, harried by a loud wind, stung his cheeks.

He glimpsed Ranulf's two companions, but forgot about them after he came into the hut. His son lived—sat upright against the backrest—had regained some weight—lifted his right arm in greeting, feebly but nonetheless lifted it!

"How have you fared?" they said into each other's mouths. Then laughter whooped from the father.

He grasped Ranulf's hand which had come alive again. That side of the face had too, was still sagging and sluggish, yet could help out in a smile . . . or a wince, as pain caused a sharply indrawn breath. "I'm sorry," Halldor said, and let go. The hand dropped to the blanket. "That was too hard for you, wasn't it?"

"I've a long way ahead before I'm hale." Ranulf's voice was also weak, and his tongue dragged a bit. "Brigit warns me that belike I'll never have my full strength back. But she thinks I will be able to get about and do enough of a man's work to earn my keep."

Halldor told himself to be glad. Aloud he answered, "Well, remember the saying of Odin:

The lame go on horseback, the handless tend herds,
The deaf are undaunted in war.
Better be blind than burnt on your pyre.
No deeds can a dead man do.

After all, if everything goes as it should, we'll be no more in viking. If you feel restless, come along on a trading voyage."

At his words, it was as though dread touched Ranulf. "Odin—" he whispered. "The One-Eyed gives such a rede, but it's he who sends battle-madness into men. . . . I do not think—" his gaze sought the crucifix—"I do not think the White Christ is that fickle."

"What do you mean?" said Halldor, taken aback. Through him stabbed the thought, *He's not even asked what happened these past days.*

"Brigit and I," said Ranulf unevenly, "we've begun talking. I've learned a few words of her speech, she more of ours—she has a quick wit—as she tended me or . . . often sat in here because I'd feel happier and mend faster if I wasn't alone, and Bjarni and Svein haven't the patience. . . . She says her God healed—is healing me. She says she could have done naught without him."

Halldor forced a shrug. "Any Christian will tell you that."

"But it must be true! What else could it be? She's cut no runes, seethed no witch-brew, called on no being save this. Though I wronged her woefully, yes, her and Christ both, I am helped—Why? They say Christ forgives those who come to him."

"They say," Halldor snapped.

"Why has he not let me die, or done what's worse and left me a breathing corpse? He must have his reasons. Shouldn't I . . . do whatever he wills . . . lest he stop helping me?" Ranulf turned eyes back toward the crucifix. "I don't want to be a cripple!"

"What do you suppose Christ does wish of you?" Halldor's tone was dull.

"I don't know." Ranulf slumped. "Father, I'm wearied. I have to sleep."

Lowering him to the bed, Halldor thought, *Well, if he takes baptism, it's not the end of the world. He'll have trouble aplenty–a householder who doesn't offer to the gods, who risks bringing down their wrath on the land–But I wonder if mostly I'm not hurt that my last son forsakes my old friend Thor.*

He may shift his mind, of course. If not . . . Brigit, you will have won that much of a victory over us.

The weather grew steadily more foul. Hailstones skittered among the rain-spears cast by a yowling, shuddering wind, to whiten an earth gone sodden. The neighbor island and the nearer mainland were well-nigh lost to sight in all that wild grey. The vikings huddled with their captives in whatever shelter was to be had.

Halldor brought his fellow skippers, Egil and

Sigurd, to his tent. Inside, it was dank and noisy and they could barely see. "I'm afraid we'll be penned here for days," he told them. "I'm not sure—who can be sure of anything about the Irish sky?—but this looks to me like the first in a long bout of springtime gales."

In such matters, they had learned to heed him. "Well," Egil said, "our wounded can use a rest ashore before we put to sea."

"And we can think over our next moves," Sigurd added. Since nothing could be known beforehand, they had laid no firm plans beyond this latest raid. Now the lower Shannon valley was picked clean. They were too few to venture on inland, where overwhelming numbers might fall on them. "Some among those folk we've taken must ken what's farther south; but beware of lies luring us into a snare."

"It's hard for a man to lie when his hand is brought above hot coals," Egil said.

"Hard, but not impossible," Halldor answered roughly. "Are the Irish less brave than the Norse? We've men dead and hurt who can tell you otherwise. No, the way to get truth is to be shrewd. Let me. I'll start by talking first with one, then another, then a third, each by himself, and marking whose tale matches whose."

He fell quiet. Rain drummed on the tent and sluiced down its sides, mists gathered within. When he was ready, he spoke anew: "Need we go on at all? We've taken a rich booty. Why not sail straight back to Armagh and sell the prisoners, and then home? They'll be in better shape. Indeed, if we cruise till the end of summer, and find no buyers earlier, we'll not only be badly crowded aboard ship but most of them will die." *Which would be a shame for them too*, he thought. *Not that I would drag out my days as a thrall. If I couldn't escape, I'd do my best to kill my owner before I was cut down. Or so I believe. Brigit might tell me I am mistaken about myself.*

Egil snorted. "What you mean, Halldor, is that your share can already pay off what you owe and leave you a stake for a fresh start in trade. Right?"

"Yes, you've heard me erenow. For yourself, though—"

"We're here for everything we can gain before winter. You swore brotherhood with us; and three ships can dare what two cannot."

Halldor hunched where he sat on the bed. The cold gnawed inward through his clothes. What might happen to Ranulf in a whole season's faring? Or himself? He did not fear death, but he would not welcome it either. Or Unn—she'd grown fat and barren, but she was still a faithful helpmeet who ought not to be left alone more than was needful.

Yet an oath was an oath. Egil's words and Sigurd's yea to them were no surprise. "As you will," Halldor sighed.

The rowing upriver, the fight at the abbey, its aftermath, the trip back through waxing storm, the meeting with his son, the work that followed, the bleakness and damp: all had worn him down. He missed Brigit when he laid himself to rest, but was too quickly asleep to fret about it.

Late in the morning he woke from a dream of her. Rain had stopped, but a stiff wind blew; the tent shook and crackled. The warmth beneath the bearskin entered his loins. He reached for her and found he was alone.

For some reason he didn't understand, he had not made use of the women the vikings lately caught. Maybe their tears had washed lust out of him. It was so much better when they also knew joy . . . . He wanted Brigit to be his in that way. He'd never before met any like her, and the strong-boned face was often in his mind. He thought it could become more alive than most women's faces, and that that would make him feel young again.

He dressed and went forth. The river was brown and wickedly choppy under a hard-driven cloud wrack. Westward loomed black-ness where lightning glimmered. He'd have had no great qualms were he at sea, but here the currents were too tricky, shores and shoals too close. Besides . . . well, Brigit had bespoken Saint Senan, the drow of this island. She'd wished a water-dragon recalled that he'd once hexed back into the deeps. What strength might his ghost still have? A storm could give it the very chance it wanted to wreak harm.

Halldor warmed his hands at a fire and got a bite to eat in one of the huts. Today he must get the loot unloaded, that it could be fairly shared out. First, however, he sought among the Irish

that had been taken at the abbey. They were
housed with their captors, in tents and throughout the monastery. The tower was unused; it
wasn't worth climbing the scaffold to shiver
amidst that icy stone. Likewise was the chapel,
also a cheerless place and maybe haunted.

Having found the man he sought, Halldor ordered, "Come along, you" in Gaelic. The fellow
stumbled sheeplike after him—young, his frame
sturdy beneath a tattered robe, but slack of jaw
and blank of eye. He'd spoken little since he was
first herded off.

As Halldor had awaited, Brigit was in the
chapel, stretched out before the altar. She had
been keeping this lonely watch, then, from the
time she saw him coming back. *And why should
she welcome me?* struck through him like a knife.
He hailed her. "Oh!" she cried, and scrambled to
her feet. Hunger and thirst had turned her pale,
but that seemed to make her shine in the dim-
ness.

She braced her shoulders as if readying herself
for a whip. "How have you fared?" she asked in a
flat voice.

He must clear his throat before he could tell
her: "The Irish had flocked to the abbey for a
stronghold. They'd raised a troop of men who
gave us a hard fight. Even after we broke them, it
was costly for us to scale the walls. No few vikings will never harass your shores again. And
. . . we will leave Scattery as soon as the
weather allows."

Still she stared at him.

"You'll have to come along, till we're sure
Ranulf is well," Halldor said awkwardly.
"Moreover, we've other wounded now that you
can help. But you have my promise you'll go free
at last. Meanwhile, uh, we've taken slaves for
market." He gestured at the silent man. "I was
careful to get a priest among them. For you,
Brigit."

She looked at the captive. The hush
lengthened below the wind outside.

"I want to make you as happy as I can,"
Halldor said, and reached for her.

She stepped back from him. "Then let me be,"
she answered.

"What?"

She did not grovel, only stood there and asked
for forbearance. "I have so much to understand,
so great a need of confession and shriving,
before—whatever else is to happen—" The spirit
flared slightly in her, like a flame out of a dying
fire. "You have new women."

He let his arm drop. After a few breaths he said
slowly: "Brigit, if it will make a difference, I
myself will spare them too. Until tomorrow—
abide in peace with your priest and your god."
He turned on his heel and walked out.

Besides unloading the ships, it would be wise
to go over them, caulking and pitching where
needed, while rain held off. If that work didn't
last till evening, he could try casting a fishline.
Afterward he'd join his men, who had taken ale
and wine on this foray as well as treasures, and
get drunk.

VIII

Eamon was the priest's name, whispered after Halldor was gone. Even so, the man cringed at every noise. Brigit wondered what he could have witnessed, to mark him so.

She wanted to be shriven, but first she must calm Father Eamon, else how might he attend to the needs of her soul? So she urged him to talk.

"I loved the ancient battle-stories," he said, "pagan though they were. Cuchulain the magnificent, mighty Finn MacCumhaill, rolling chariots, prancing horses, sun sheening off spears that men kissed before battle—but it wasn't like that at all, at all, Sister Brigit. A lad clutched his spilling guts, fell to his knees and screamed and screamed until he was nothing but screaming. And the blood! I've seen blood as much as most, but never did I wade through lakes of it, and that of my neighbors and kin.

"We thought the walls would hold them off, even after our warriors were beaten, but they'd brought ladders to scale the palisades, and they stationed men at the souterrain exits, so none could escape. At last we saw the end of hope. We cried out to Patrick, Mary, and to God Himself, but none answered but the yelling, grinning Lochlannach.

"Old Abbot Niall tried to halt them at the

church door. The Sacrament was yet inside.
They split his head and trod across his body. His
bones cracked, one by one, until he lay a shape-
less mass of red. They scattered the Sacred Host
underfoot.

"A few tried to stand fast in a storeroom. The
Lochlannach fired it. I still can smell the reek of
roasting flesh and barley."

Screams outside mixed with laughter. Brigit
and Eamon looked out the door. Nearby several
men were tumbling a woman in the mud. The
woman spat at Brigit.

Eamon closed his eyes and shuddered. "When
all was lost, and we made submission, they did
that to my wife. I was bound, and could not help
her. She would not submit; she wailed and
struggled. I heard bones snap. They must have
decided that, wounded, she'd be no use as a
slave. After all were finished, the last ravisher
stuck his knife in her." And then, a howl, *"Where
was Christ?"*

Brigit thought Eamon's wife had been lucky.
She touched him on the arm. That she should
offer comfort to a priest . . . "Surely she awaits
you in Heaven."

"The way she glared at me—I never can forget.
I could not rescue her, but always I see those
eyes. How could I ever face her again?" He wept.
"God has turned His face away and left us to the
demons."

"You must *never* say any such thing. Despair
is the greatest sin." The woman outside had
stopped shrieking; Brigit heard only keening and

coarse laughter. Well she remembered; she felt anew the fullness of her breasts and the heaviness in her belly. Yet she, too, was unable to avenge yon woman. Her helplessness gagged her.

Eamon gave her a mad smile. "And you, sister, for all your brave words, have you never despaired?"

Brigit flushed. "I'd be grateful if you would shrive me. Long has it been, and much has happened." He heard out her catalogue of sins, such as she told. It seemed his mind wandered as he murmured absolution.

Dusk thickened. Outside Brigit heard drunken revelry. Of course, the Lochlannach must celebrate! She dared not leave the chapel. Here was a fellow Christian in need, and Halldor had cause to be wroth with her.

She watched with Eamon, and tried to pray. The priest spent much of his time staring into darkness, or mumbling senseless Latin phrases. A great shout rose from the campfire—one of the crew must have made a foolhardy boast—and Eamon cast himself to the dirt, trembling. *Forgive him, dear God, that he no longer is a man.* She sat against the chapel wall. The stones were chill on her back. When she dozed she saw her father again, as a young man, felt him toss her high in the air and laugh. She huddled in the rustling dark and heard her mother's tales of the Sídhe, those who dwell in the dolmens. She was a novice, pledging her body and life to Christ—she woke with a snap. The chapel was black, and in the darkness she heard whimpering. *What has Eamon seen that is worse than I've survived?* She stumbled over in the dark to comfort him with a touch and a few words, but he only curled into a tighter ball.

Brigit rose. The cold struck through her garments, rain spattered through the open door, and the House of God stank of mildew. She could bear no more. Halldor, at least, was warm. His hands were not always nailed to a cross.

She bowed against the storm as she walked to his tent.

IX

She woke him when she crept into bed and cuddled at his side, but almost at once she was asleep. He lay quiet and wondered what it meant. Merely that she was chilled? No, she could have curled up with her back to him and a space between, as always before. She might call herself a humble handmaiden of Christ, but her inner pride was as stark as any Norsewoman's. Had she, then, gotten the same lust for him that he'd been carrying for her? That thought nearly made him take hold of her and mount. He reined himself in. She was worn out. Let her rest.

What need for haste? Nobody was going anywhere today. Let him woo her.

After he had long enjoyed the feel of her flesh against his, he rose. First he picked up the drenched garb she had cast off and hung it on a hook at the ridgepole to dry as much as it might. Throwing a cloak across his shoulders—the pin that fastened it was Irish—he unlaced the doorflap. A fire was banked in a small pit just outside, roofed by interwoven boughs on four stakes. He kindled a splint among the coals and took that back inside to light a brazier. Soon the edge was off the air. Food and drink were stowed here, for it behooved a chieftain to offer them to anyone who came calling. He sliced beef and cooked it on a spit.

The smell seemed to reach Brigit. She sat up.

As they left the bearskin, her rosy-tipped breasts seemed to light the gloom. A short brown curl fell endearingly across her brow. "Good morning," he greeted. "You must be starved. Shall we break our fast?"

She smiled—then, as full awareness came, stiffened.

"Don't fear me." Halldor pushed the meat into a trencher and sat down on the bedside. His palm stroked the softness of her cheek on its way to cup her chin and draw the grey eyes toward him. "You deserve well."

She bridled. "I've received little thus far."

"You'll have your freedom in due course, as I've often said. And return to your father's hall if you wish. And, maybe, friendship between him and me that will safeguard you. Unless—" Halldor stopped for a few heartbeats. "Unless you'd rather—" He broke off. "But let's eat."

She saw what he had done and was astounded. "You readied a meal—*you* are serving *me*?"

He nodded.

The food made an inner glow, the ale more so. It must have gone straight to Brigit's hunger-smitten head, for she leaned back on an elbow, after the last bite was sunken and the horns refilled, and spoke fast:

"Halldor, you've vowed to provide for me. Will you for my child?"

"What?" he barked.

This time her smile lasted. "Have you not noticed? And you a family man. I am with child."

Mine, Ranulf's, any of six or seven others—nobody will ever know chased through him.

"I, I can do nothing for it if you stay behind," he stammered.

In an upward storm—how fair she was!—he cast forth: "But Brigit, if you'll come with me to Norway, I'll acknowledge it as my own. And there'll be more afterward, strong sons and daughters. A leman-child has no drawbacks under the law in my land. Unn would be glad of such fresh timbers for our house, she'd welcome you—"

My own head is likewise a-buzz, he fleetingly knew.

"You offer me more than God has done," she told him in a slurred tone.

He threw off the cloak and sought her. She did not lie waiting to suffer him, but cast arms around his neck. Because of that, and because of recalling how, earlier, she had once or twice halfway come to life here, Halldor went slowly and gently, feeling his way forward to whatever might please her. When at last he cried out, she did too.

X

Brigit gasped, not because Halldor's weight was painful. She trembled and held him close. So this was the pleasure she'd vowed never to know. But her vows were shattered.

He leaned on his elbow, tensed, as if afraid to cause pain, then eased off her. She curled against him and flung one arm across his back. She tried to keep her eyes open, tried to say something, but her vision blurred and she could not speak. After the chill vigil of the night before, the food and drink conspired. His breath misted warm on her face. She drowsed.

She woke—how much later—minutes? hours?—to find Halldor half-sitting, looking down at her. In the yellow light she could not read his expression.

So it was not in the embrace of the living God I found my joy. The guilt was less than she'd expected. But what must Halldor think? She had held nothing back, she had cried out, clawed him like an animal. She felt her face go red, and drew the furs up around her neck.

Halldor reached forth and stroked her cheek with a blunt finger. Rough it was, calloused from oars and ropes and swords, but his touch was gentle. "Brigit, Brigit." His palm moved to her hair. "Joy becomes you. Never were you meant for a nun."

She dared to look at him. His brow furrowed. He leaned toward her. She stretched out a hand and noticed how it shook. "Halldor—"

She never knew what she would have said next; a clamor rose outside. The words were Norse, and Brigit did not understand, but Halldor cursed, sprang from the bed, and threw his cloak about him.

The news was bad, Brigit knew. More slowly, she dressed and followed him.

A ragged group of men had gathered at the shore. They peered across the choppy water. In the mist, at the limit of vision, a man's head bobbed. He swam slowly, and the current swept him seaward. The head went under, and reappeared only once.

Brigit drew back from the others. Halldor stood, his cloak flapping in the wet wind. Two men pointed to the river, then to the chapel, and shook their heads. Grimfaced, Halldor heard them out. They gestured to one of the ships.

"No," he said. Turning away, he caught sight of Brigit. He stepped near and clasped her shoulder. "It was the priest, Eamon," he said in her tongue.

"Eamon?" Brigit saw how she had left him: collapsed on the chapel floor, despairing. She had walked from him to Halldor's tent, Halldor's bed, of her free will. She should pray for Eamon's soul, but her prayers would be sacrilege. "What happened?"

"He ran from the chapel, screaming like a berserker, straight for the river. The guards could not stop him. They had no idea he meant to swim. The current here is swift, the water chill—"

This was no escape attempt. Eamon had taken his own life while she lay in sin with Halldor.

She stared across the Shannon. The fog that veiled the sun swirled sullen over the wave-tops: the grey of oblivion. Eamon had gone *gealt,* of course. The horrors he had witnessed had deranged him. And, after all, what future had he faced? His God had abandoned him. He would live out his days as a pagan's thrall, in a foreign land—if, indeed, he survived the summer.

And at the end, in that cold building, no one answered. No God, nor even his countrywoman. I lay abed with my captor, and took pleasure in it. Brigit brushed Halldor's hand from her shoulder and strode toward Ranulf's hut.

Ranulf raised on his good elbow when Brigit

came through the door. "What was the shout-
ing?"

"A thrall tried to flee. He drowned."

"Oh." Ranulf lay back. Brigit made ready for
the bathing and exercise. "He go . . . to Heaven
. . . to Christ?"

"I fear he will not. He broke God's law."

Ranulf's eyes were bright. "What is God's
law?"

"Am I a priest that should be telling you?" She
bit back rage and tears. "Come, let's get to

work." She was more brisk with his exercises than was her wont. When she bent his knee he gasped. Exasperated, she said, "Shall I spare you pain, and let you lie abed a cripple all your life?" After that he kept silent.

As she finished, Halldor came to the door and stood looking in. "His limbs move freer, Brigit. Well have you wrought."

She gathered up the basin and cleansing-cloths, and looked into his blue eyes. She read pain there.

"Brigit—" He reached toward her. "I'm sorry about your friend." But he stood now fully dressed. His mantle was clasped with the stolen brooch, and she remembered fires across her land.

"I regret the drowning of your property, my lord." She waited until he stepped aside, then brushed past carrying the basin. *So near*—her arm touched his tunic, and she trembled. She hastened from the hut.

She'd washed the rags and hung them on bushes, though in such grey wind she doubted they would dry. The longer her body kept busy, the longer her mind might keep still.

At last she lifted her head, threw back her shoulders, and began to walk along the beach. The tide had turned, and with it the Shannon current shifted. Where a sweep of gravel curled into the water, she saw the dark and sodden corpse hooked onto a root.

*I'll not be burying you in consecrated ground,
brother Christian, father priest, for you're a suicide.* And she could scarcely bury him in any
case. She dragged the body up the bank and
heaped a cairn above it. She said no prayers nor
raised any cross.

Rage drove her to the holy well. Moss-
bordered and clear, it mirrored the leaden sky.
She crouched near its edge. If she closed her eyes
she could see Halldor's face, and her body still

remembered Halldor's touch. *Shall I go back, then, and live as his leman?* But beside Halldor she saw the drowned face of the priest. Behind Halldor smoke curled above the fields, and through his laugh she heard captives weeping. Her fist clutched a stone. *He has taken my body, he has killed my people and plundered my land— he has even bent my soul—and I would lie beside him?* She flung the stone into the pool.

Water struck her face like tears. She clenched her fists until her palms bled. *"Damn them,"* she screamed, *"damn them all, damn Halldor!* My curse on him, my curse on all his folk. May their ships founder, may monsters claw them down beneath the waves, may they swill salt beer at their wake!" She sobbed.

Crows clamored from the rowan tree; invisible gulls screeched, and then all birds were gone. The mist swirled silent.

Brigit felt a cool hand on her shoulder. "Daughter, do you mean your curse?" The voice was like music. Brigit raised her head. Her lashes must carry tears, for the woman she saw was wreathed in rainbows: tall, golden-haired, gold-crowned, the woman in her dream. "Do you truly curse Halldor and all his following?"

Brigit shrank back. This might be a holy well, but here stood no saint. The Brigit of her namesake had been an abbess. No abbess would wear a sea-green mantle whose shimmer mirrored waves, nor would her habit be spun of spider-silk. "Yes, I am Brigit," the woman said.

"But you cannot be. The Brigit I called was a nun, even as I am—was."

"Before *that* Brigit there was another. I am that one, and this well is mine. But answer me, do you truly mean your curse?"

Do I curse Halldor? Blue eyes crinkled at the corners. Far-flung mind. Hands skilled at carpentry and—other things. Her blood seethed. "Halldor and his men have ravaged the land, slain my people, brought me shame—"

"Shame, is it now you're calling it?" The rainbow woman laughed. "Strange folk, Christians. But you have given me reasons, not answers. Do you truly ill-wish the Lochlannach? Do you will that evil befall them? For if you wish, so will it be. They are none of my land."

Halldor. The rest could perish, but—She closed her eyes and saw slaughtered monks, flies buzzing round their bodies. She heard sobbing captives, remembered bruises and blows, and felt the ache in her own breasts. Halldor led these men. She swallowed, and said, "I *do* curse them. I *do* ill-wish them, each and every one. Would that Saint Senan—"

"Strange for you to prate of saints," the woman said, "on this Bealtaine Eve. Your mother taught you the old ways, Brigit. She spoke true. Place your curse with care."

The rainbow blurred, and the woman vanished. Where she had stood was merely a patch of green moss, like any other spot on the banks of the pool. The crows noised back into the rowan

tree.

Bealtaine. She'd been a small child, then. In later years the abbess taught her to call it May Day, or Lady Day, for it was now a feast of the Blessed Virgin, and pagan practices were not to be borne. But she recalled standing with her mother, scattering yellow primroses on the threshold of her father's chamber. His wife, going toward her lawful bed, kicked them aside. "Ignorant heathen."

Brigit's mother had swept the blooms into her

apron, and Brigit cried. "Can it be she does not wish him safe from harm this night?"

"Hush, child. She'll be rising early enough to draw first well-water, for all her proud ways. Come with me, now, and make sure the fire is out, lest some ill-wisher steal a coal."

These, Brigit was later taught, were the ways of bondfolk and servants. Her mother, dead, had not been able to gainsay the abbess. Now, though, she breathed the cool air, and felt the sun warm her hands and face. Beneath her feet the island throbbed with power. In the distance the river chuckled, the wind whispered.

It was the river and the wind that would avenge her. As a Bealtaine gift she'd present Halldor with a charm. A simple charm to bring him luck on his next voyage.

Greyly, *but he will trust me, and be destroyed.* Then she laughed. *The land, and I, and my people will have revenge. Let the weak show mercy. The weak die.*

No need to pick flowers for the doorways, nor gaud a May-bush; tonight she had no desire to ward off harm. And for today she'd best perform her duties, appear calm, beware of rousing any suspicion.

Again she tended Ranulf. He needed little help with his feeding, and he'd regained enough control that he need not be swaddled. He was healing more rapidly than expected. Not that this would do him any good, after tomorrow. She

fended off his questions of Christ; why had she
ever cared about his soul? Having hurried
through her tasks, she departed.

Nothing drew her toward the scriptorium.
Learning was part of her former life. She wished
darkness would fall.

Halldor was out with the men, sorting and
storing plunder. It should be safe to return to the
tent. She was cold and wet.

Brigit pulled aside the tent-flap. There, on the
bed, lay a blue gown, a scarlet mantle, and a
jeweled belt. Women's clothes—Halldor must
have brought them. But as she felt the soft thick
stuff she thought of how he'd gotten it. No matter, that; she was ashiver. She cast aside her
nun's habit and donned the garments. The thick
wool lay warm against her skin. When she had
stopped trembling, she combed her hair. In a few
months it would be long enough again to braid,
if she lived.

About mid-afternoon the mist scattered before
a brisk wind. Men spread cloaks and bedding to
dry. Their mood became festive. It was time to
stow their gear and make everything ready. Tomorrow they would move on along the coast.

Food they had a-plenty; no need to carry it all.
Why not hold a feast? They could get more
wherever they landed. The countryside was rich,
and summer was young.

Slaves had the meal ready by twilight. Fire
gleamed off the men's arm-rings and brace-

lets—*stolen gold*—and wine and ale flowed freely.

Brigit sought the serving women, though they
glared at her and muttered. Only the young and
comely had been taken. She knew what had be-
fallen the infirm and those heavy with child. She
gave them no sign, and carried food to Halldor.

He smiled. "Brigit! Get yourself a bowlful, and
sit beside me, here!"

"If you will it, lord," she said. And so finally
tonight she sat by his side and smiled, even when

the vikings gaped in astonishment, even when the Irishwomen made evil signs in her direction. *Nothing must betray me.*

She handed Halldor a four-handled silver *mether.* He took the opposite handle and drank deep, then passed it back to her. His eyes crinkled; she smiled over the rim of her cup and gulped the wine.

When one of the crew seized a serving-wench and tumbled her in front of the others, she leaned closer to Halldor. He glanced at her, wondering, no doubt, if she'd take it ill. Brigit rested her head on his shoulder. *Let him think it is the wine.*

"Long have you camped on this island, lord," she said, carefully slurring her words, "but never have you honored its own spirits."

"Do you mean your saints?" Halldor only half-listened. The wench was putting up a good fight.

"No, no, not the saints. The spirits of the land. Tomorrow is Bealtaine, for shame, and you taking no notice."

Others of the crew were moving in. Halldor shook his head and looked at Brigit. "In a day or so we'll be gone."

She cuddled closer. "Ah, but this island is special. Have you never noticed how it commands the river? It's a tradition among my people to sail *tuathal* around it on Bealtaine, that their boats may be blessed and their voyages lucky." Such was partially true—but the tradition was

to sail *deisal*, with the sun, for fortune. *Tuathal*—anti-sunward—was for undoing, dark deeds, and evil. And to set sail at all on Bealtaine—

Halldor regarded her with interest. "Do they indeed? Why do you tell me?"

As if in response, Brigit drew closer. "You fare off soon on fresh adventures, and have you not said you'd take me along, that I might care for your son and the other wounded? Little would I wish to see your ships accursed!"

"Right enough," said Halldor. He gnawed a shred of meat and threw the bone into the fire. Else he made no move.

He does not quite believe me. He is no fool. "I did not care, earlier, what happened," she went on. "What matter if I lived or died? But now—" She smiled at him and rested both hands on her belt.

He shrugged. "I've never been given to overmuch dread of the land-wights, wherever I went." Thoughtfully: "And yet these *are* Irish waters, and if you yourself, a Christian, give me such a rede—" He shook himself and made a wry smile. "If nothing else, the men could gain added heart from hearing we'll do what we can to make our peace with the Powers hereabouts. Well, I'll ask my fellow skippers what they think. Meanwhile, Brigit, best you hie off to bed. Whatever we do tomorrow, it will be early. From the sky tonight, the weather should be fair. Best to snatch that chance whenever it happens by, in Ireland!"

Yes, best, passed through Brigit. *It'll be the last day you ever see.* She bade him a meek goodnight and left. From the tent-flap she watched as he sought his two captains and, she supposed, explained matters. One—Egil, she recognized, master of *Reginleif*—seemed to ask a question. Halldor answered merrily, and all three men whooped with laughter. Nodding their heads, the two slapped Halldor on the back and left him.

When he came to her that night Brigit feigned

warmth, but inwardly her flesh was ice. When at last he slept she stared into darkness. From time to time she rose to tend the fire. Tonight it must not burn out. She had a use for it.

A brightening eastern sky woke the first birds. Brigit looked across at sleeping Halldor. Peaceful, he seemed, his mouth relaxed in a faint smile, the creased, leathery skin almost smooth. Slowly she eased herself from bed and dressed against the chill. The coals yet glowed beneath their shell of ash. She blew one to yellow light and thrust in a splint. There, it flickered and caught. She stood. "With this fire I take the luck out of this house," she whispered, and stepped from the tent. A breeze blew from the west, and she must shield the flame with her new cloak. None stirred but nightwatch; they sat sleepy, marked her passing, and nodded again. No reason why Halldor's woman might not walk to the river.

Waves licked the pebbled shore. Clear heavens and lively air boded well for sailors. Brigit stood ankle-deep and stared at the wavering flame. "This brand is the luck of Halldor's house, and the luck of all his crew. As it is snuffed out, so may they be." There was a hiss as she plunged it into the water. She drew forth a charred and dripping stick. "So be it." She flung it from her, rose, and went back to the tent.

On her way she noticed the grass was heavy with dew. Young girls would collect Maydew to

bathe their faces, that they grow beautiful. But what use had Brigit for beauty? Her feet left dull tracks through the sparkle.

She had not been visiting Ranulf at daybreak. If she were found missing, Halldor might wonder. She paused at the monastery well to draw a bucket of water before anyone else could. "Again, ill-luck upon this house." She poured the water on the ground. Having filled the bucket anew she returned with it to Halldor's tent.

He must have heard her come in, for he roused. "You're up betimes, Brigit. It's hardly light."

"On Bealtaine," she said, "it's lucky to draw first water. Here, I have brought you a drink." She dipped a cup in the bucket and held it out.

He gulped deep. "Ah, thanks." Raising an eyebrow: "Is all this—the water, the sailing— lore you learned from books?"

Brigit shook her head. "None of this is written."

"Hm—yes, I daresay your clerics frown on what men do to stay friends with the elves. Though it is wise—at least, no harm in it—the more so for us, who have White Christ for a foe. I'm glad you told me of this." He reached for her. "But you've done your share now." He laughed. "Come and be warmed."

The thought was horrible. "Have we time? It's best you sail early in the day."

"We've time." He pulled her to him. She pretended to enjoy. Within, she shuddered. In a few hours the arms that held her would stretch cold and dead.

Men thronged the shore. Only one turn about
the island? No great task, that; then they could
spend the rest of the day preparing to leave. If
this charm would help them later, why, wonderful! Waves and wind were always chancy things.

Brigit kept well away from where the captives
were housed, and hoped none would betray her.
Surely they suspected what she meant to do.

"You'll sail with us, Brigit?" Halldor said.
"After all, you go on the voyage."

She shook her head. "I fear a boat ride today, over the waves—" With a hand to her forehead she swayed slightly, as if close to fainting. "I would be ill. Soon enough when I *must* travel." Halldor reached out to steady her. "I shall watch from shore," she said. "Best that you lead your captains and the crews. Yours is the ordering of all; to you should come the greatest part of the luck."

Swiftly, then, were the ships pushed into deeper water. Bright the striped sails bellied. To sail *tuathal* around this island in shifting wind would be a test of seamanship, but the crews were skilled. Laughing, with sail and oar they set out.

Brigit watched and waited for their doom.

First they drew well offshore, and she remembered Halldor remarking that he always tried to have plenty of sea room. Of course, here he was not in the sea where he belonged—*Would God he had never come from it, for his own sake, even. But I am no longer God's handmaid, am I? At least not that God. Nor am I Halldor's lover.* The farther he went from Scattery's desolation, the nearer he came to the mainland that lay so heartbreakingly green and peaceful-looking. In mid-channel, *Sea Bear* came about. *Shark* and *Reginleif* made the same move in her wake, with less ease. Well, less-skilled hands were on their helms.

They needed all the skill they owned, yon steersmen. Though the current was with them at

this start of their round trip, the hitherto favorable airs were swinging—strengthening, too, heartbeat by heartbeat as Brigit stood on a hillock above the strand and gazed outward. She saw yardarms hauled around, sails poled out, and even then marveled at how gracefully the dragons danced over the waves.

Whitecaps suddenly sprang to life on the great brown stream. The wind raised them faster than she had ever seen it happen before, surely faster than Halldor himself ever had. Louder and louder it shrilled, strained with chill fingers at her gown as if it too would ravish her; and more and more it became westerly, streaking straight up the Shannon to overflow this island and everything around. She stood yet in sunlight, but it had grown wan; the very sun seemed to flicker in the blast. Up over the western horizon clouds lifted fast enough to see. They became a blue-black wall. Lightning blazed more bright and swift than flames from a burning homestead. Thunder rolled across miles. It sounded like the wheels of a giant chariot. *But it is not his Thor who rules this storm. Mananaan Mac Lir is rising now in wrath.* The first flung raindrops stung Brigit's face. She felt herself grin. *Halldor the Weatherwise did not foresee* this *gale.*

She must squint and shield eyes with hands to make out how the ships fared. They had gone surprisingly far while her thoughts blew about in her; they were almost out of her sight near the head of the island, distance-dwindled to toys.

(For an instant she wondered if Halldor had
carved a toy boat for Ranulf when the boy was
little. Of course he had.) Doubtless the Lochlannach would reckon it shame, and unlucky as
well, to give way before a mere squall. She made
out how the hulls pitched and yawed. Their
brave coloring of sails had been struck. Oars
labored spidery. Not long ago Halldor had tried
to render into Gaelic one of his own poems for
her. It bespoke his ship as "the many-footed
dragon of the swan's bath—"

Brigit strained to look west. Thence would come revenge. The storm-blackness had engulfed half of heaven, and still boiled onward. Ahead of it, wrack covered the rest. The light that trickled through was the color of brass, hard to see by; and the lightning flares beyond dazzled her eyes, left blue-white images in her vision. Yet when the thing appeared she knew.

For an instant, terror gripped her. She had not thought to ask herself what form the anger of the land would take. Enough that her namesake, the goddess whom the Christians had tried to make a saint, had promised. Maybe Lugh of the Long Hand would come in his chariot with his terrible beauty, spear lifted on high; maybe the Morrigan would lead her shrieking troop of witches upon the wind—

What swam from the sea toward the ships was longer than any hull. Foam seethed around the serpent coils. Lightning-light shimmered along the ebon scales. High as a dragon figurehead reared the tapering snout, flickering tongue, glistening small eyes. Jaws gaped; against the murk behind, Brigit could see how cold seafire dripped from the fangs and was whipped away on the blast.

She knew. *This was Saint Senan's island, whence he drove the monster and which he made holy by his prayers. But his work has been undone, the last consecrate has forsworn Christ, the Old Ones are astir, and Cata the frightful is coming home again.*

These Lochlannach, at least, would harry her country no more. A joy seized her, Cuchulain's battle joy. She raised her arms aloft and cried into the wind, "Welcome, Cata! A hundred thousand welcomes!"

The air roared and roiled. Darkness deepened save for the firebolts that leaped among the clouds. Thunder banged as though from within her skull, rain came flying like arrows, and she could see no more across the water.

XI

At first Halldor had not been alarmed, only angered. Hell take this Irish weather! Loki himself ruled over it. Every sign had been good. Well, he'd seen enough of its tricksiness not to be taken much aback, and so quick a blow ought not to get dangerous in the time his band would use for rounding the main island. (Watch out for the lesser eyot, though, when they'd nearly have drawn the lucky circle to a close. Passage through the strait between it and Scattery would be almost as trying as to go north of it with the mainland for a lee shore beyond.)

Then the storm waxed, swifter than Odin's eight-legged horse galloped of nights in the Wild Hunt. Sails fought the men who would lower and furl them, cloth flapped and snapped, loose ends of lines whipped blood from skin. Murk and lightning boiled up out of the west and over the sky. Wind raved, thrust, snatched at *Sea Bear*'s hull so that she kept veering broadside to; only her oarsmen brought her back in time, wielding their blades with all their strength in answer to commands Halldor bawled from the

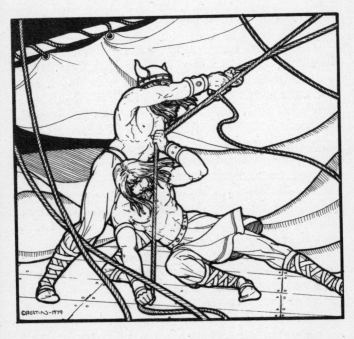

rudder. Belike the racket around and crash above often drowned him out—but they were stout lads, they knew the sea and its ways—but this wasn't the sea, the whitecaps were becoming waves with no two alike, tide and gale and river-flow made currents, rips, chop like none he had ever met before—Through the rain and hail that began to drive about him, he saw how *Reginlief* and *Shark* lurched. Masts, which there had not been a chance to take down, swayed crazily against half-seen forest which the lightning whitened. The pennons at all their heads were torn off.

The ships must find shelter, else they'd likeliest be wrecked. Halldor squinted landward. He could barely make out what lay there, but didn't think that a safe place to beach was any part of it. Yonder was miry, reedy ground, where a hull could stick fast and be battered to pieces. Wisest would be to steer for Scattery: the south end, away from a Hog Island which had become a trap, then up along the eastern side, where the wind ought to be lessened. Maybe they could reach the haven they'd left. Or maybe they'd have to ride at anchor, which they could hardly do here, until the gale quieted.

Either way, they'd finish the lap that Brigit had said would bless them! Halldor laughed and shouted his orders. Sigurd and Egil could see from their craft what he was doing and followed his lead.

It would take seamanship to turn without being caught between weather and water. Halldor lifted his left hand off the tiller, to wave signals that would let his oarsmen work together.

Then out of the rage ahead came the monster.

It stabbed through Halldor: *The Midgard Snake. The Weird of the World is upon us, and the gods themselves must die.* Wreathed with rain and lightning, the great head seemed to lift into heaven, the writhing black coils to churn up the deeps. Was the storm really Thor on his way to meet it, slay and be slain?

A sheet of blue-white fire across most of the sky limned it against tossing trees ashore. His sailor's eyes took the size from that. No, it could not have lain on the bottom as a belt around the world—and no Fimbul Winter of three years' length had foretold its arising, though today might well be the ax-time, sword-time, wind-time, wolf-time that the spaewife had said would come first. . . . Yonder snake-thing was as long as any ship men could build, surely many tons heavier. But no more.

No matter. It could kill him and his crew as dead as if it did bring the end of everything that is.

It was bearing straight at *Sea Bear*, but not very fast. Maybe, maybe the men could outrow it; maybe it could not go on land. What else was there to do but try? Fear still made an ice-lump at Halldor's core, for it is not easy to meet a troll; and what mightier Powers had loosed this one? But he mastered himself; his inwardness grew altogether cool and steady, and he gave all his mind to that which must be done.

The bow lookout had likewise seen, and stumbled back screaming. He fell off the foredeck, down among the benches. Men missed their strokes, the ship lost headway. "Row, you scoundrels!" Halldor bellowed. The loudness tore at his gullet. "Bend to it, by the Hammer!"—*if you'd have any hope of living*, a whisper added from within. They heard, they saw him

stand firm at the helm and send his bidding to them, the habit of years took hold and they laid themselves into the task.

Not even as the ship was coming around and everybody saw the beast did they waver much. A rainbow shimmer ran across its scales. They thought that through wind-howl and rain-rush they could hear a monstrous hissing. Yet they brought their vessel about and raised waves of their own as they bore back upstream.

Current was against them now, but the gale with them. For a trice Halldor wished they could spare time to raise sail anew. But no—this water was too treacherous, too narrow—and whoever ruled the storm could aim it any way he chose— In the end, a man had naught to count on but his own strength. Halldor began the old chant, *"Tyr hold us, ye Tyr, ye Odin–"* His men took it up, not loudly for they had no breath to spare, but letting it fill them and be the drumbeat that ordered their strokes.

Halldor glanced to starboard and saw that *Reginleif* was also headed for Scattery. Where was *Shark*? Sudden horror on the faces below made him twist his neck to peer aft.

A cry broke from him. *Shark* had been too awkward, had gone afoul of wind and riptides and barely made her turn before she was swamped. Those aboard who were not rowing were madly bailing, but she wallowed sluggish. The worm had changed course toward her.

It was upon her.

Its forepart reared over the sternpost. The head came weaving forward. A crewman dropped his bailer and thrust with a spear. The head darted, mouth agape. Through the rain driving against him, Halldor thought he could see that a fang, the size of a forearm, barely wounded the sailor through his shirt. Yet that man let go his weapon, clutched his belly, and fell. Poison—

The head withdrew. Then, more slowly, those grinning jaws lowered again. They closed on the

helmsman, the skipper. Halldor glimpsed how
limbs sprattled as the snake arched its neck on
high. Blood welled and was lost in the river.
Sigurd passed from sight, swallowed whole:
Sigurd Tryggvason, friend in this faring, troll-
food.

Shark drifted helpless. Some of her folk sprang
overboard, some snatched for their fighting
gear. It made no difference. The snake picked
them from either place. Iron did not bite on
those scales. After it had taken four or five, it

attacked the ship herself. Snout battered, coils
lashed and heaved. The mast broke, the dragon
head tumbled off, ribs and strakes gave way.
Sigurd's proud craft became flotsam drifting
down the Shannon. The beast hunted about, kill-
ing swimmers with bites and blows. It did not
eat any more. There should be ample feeding
later. It moved on upstream after the rest.

All this had Halldor witnessed in stolen
glances. Mainly he must keep aware of the ever-
changing forces that ramped about him, hold
Sea Bear on course with his own oar and his
men's. By the time *Shark* was done for, Scattery
Island loomed near.

He changed his mind about where to steer.
The northern passage was tricky but the lesser
holm and the closer mainland shore made a
weaker current for his wearying rowers to buck.
Besides, that way they would sooner reach the
bay, where he knew they could safely ground.

To slant across the river toward the strait took
the whole of Halldor's skill. Egil on *Reginleif*
tried the same, but could not do it so well. His
ship fell ever farther aft. The snake drew ever
closer, until plain was to see that he would not
escape.

Across tumbling waters and lashing, hail-
edged rain, Egil waved at Halldor. What he
shouted did not carry through the gale, but his
own crew must have heard, for they wielded
their oars as one and *Reginleif* came around. Like
a flung spear, she sprang to meet her foe.

She rammed straight into the huge form and swung to lay alongside. Swords, axes, spears flashed across the rail. The snake looped clear, unhurt, lowered its head, and reaped among the vikings. Thereafter it wrecked their hull and slew whoever was left. "But you made a good ending, Egil, you and your carls," breathed Halldor.

They had kept the troll from him, too, while he rounded the northern spit and bore toward haven. Belike Egil had died hoping that Halldor would get home to tell his saga.

Dim on the starboard quarter, save when lightning flared to turn the slant of rain steel-grey, the tower now rose in sight. And the monster also did, threshing through the river. "We're almost there," Halldor said to himself; and aloud, as loudly as he was able: "Row, row! Thrandheim waits for us!"

The bay, the strand—the monk-huts beyond, and Ranulf lay in one of them—and Brigit abode there too—Had she witched forth the worm? She was no common kind of woman, and she had much to avenge. But—On! Drive *Sea Bear* up the shallows till her keel shocks home! Overboard, into the stream, drag her higher while Thor's hammer smites with fire and his goats draw the thunder-car rumbling over heaven!

Men stumbled onto what had been dry land, where rainwater swirled and gurgled around their feet. Halldor led them in making the ship fast. Without this last of the three, they were

doomed anyway. As for the snake, if it could not come ashore, it could not move in the yard or less of depth where she lay.

Suddenly Halldor grew aware that when he left her he had not taken his ax along. Instead, he had snatched his own hammer from beneath the foredeck, where he had returned it after the offering. Well, no weapon forged by man would help in this plight, while the tool had hitherto always brought him luck in his farings. He picked it up from the ground, having dropped it there so he might have both hands free to haul on a mooring line. The weight in his grasp was strangely heartening. He looked outward.

Hugeness waved back and forth through the river, the head on high darted back and forth through rain. Forlorn, the Norse huddled in their sodden clothes, gripped hafts gone slippery with wetness, and waited to learn their lot. The thing had seen them. It turned. Slowly, as if wanting to keep them unknowing, it swam closer.

Halldor could not tell whether he heard or felt that length grate upon shingle. He did see that the giant kept on coming. More and more of its barrel rippled above water. It slid past the ship; its first coil crossed the meeting of water and island.

Somebody wailed. Somebody else broke into a run. All at once the whole crew bolted, right, left, inland, anywhere. Halldor stood alone. The snake bore on up toward him.

XII

Wind-driven waves lashed the island, and rain made Brigit's gown a clammy shroud. Hailstones stung her face and hands. Some drew blood, but she paid no heed. Off in the river, in lightning-driven darkness, battle raged.

A flash revealed the monster, its neck arched. Another flash showed a sheared mast, a splintered hull, men thrashing overboard. Darkness for a time; when lightning flared again the battle had moved closer. Again the beast reared, as a ship rammed it. Brigit clenched her fists. They eased when she recognized *Reginleif*. *That was well done. I must grant the Lochlannach courage.*

But what of Halldor? And what is it to me if he lies dead by my witchery? Another bolt replied: *Sea Bear* had made harbor. Through the murk she saw men haul the ship aground, and heard, amid storm, the scrape of wood on gravel. *So. He lives yet, and the battle comes ashore.*

Running, scrambling, shouts, and behind it all, a slithering. Sick light gleamed through cloud-shreds, and Brigit saw: the thing was nigh as thick as she stood tall, and stretched, it seemed, out to infinity. Might rippled beneath the gleaming black scales as the creature slid onto land.

The crew scattered. Only Halldor stood his ground. The beast held its head high, paused, balanced as if choosing, then darted forth at a

fleeing man. It drew back to wait, but the man was already down, pierced by a fang as long as Brigit's forearm. One of Ranulf's gang, the man had been. He lay still, and the rest of them fled every which way. Daintily, the beast engulfed its prey and swallowed him whole. It raised its neck and looked around for more. The lidless gaze fixed on Halldor.

Alone in the tempest, Halldor seemed absurdly small. The creature flowed across the ground. A coil looped near where Brigit stood. Each scale was as large as her palm; she could not see over the crested back. The thing was close enough that she could smell its stink: musk and corruption and death. She retreated, hand over mouth. "The Serpent from Eden," she breathed. "My God, what have I raised?" Muscles bunched and the sleek side brushed her. She screamed and fled toward camp.

Rain blinded her, or was it tears? She tripped and sprawled. Her hands scoured across gravel; the pain shocked her, brought her back. *Coward. You summoned it. Face what you have done.*

The monster had turned from Halldor and was stalking her. Unhuman eyes, slit-pupilled, stared. The tongue flicked. It held its head aloft, eager, questing.

She freed her feet from her tangled skirt and made ready to flee again. Then she remembered: when the vikings bolted, Cata had chosen one. When she ran, it tracked her. She tried not to breathe.

At the edge of sight she tallied what lay beyond

her: mostly barren ground. The nearest refuge
was Ranulf's hut, and beyond that the chapel.
From inside it, through the wind and enormous
rustling of scales, she could hear screams,
prayers, and lamentation. That would be the
Irish captives; they'd sought sanctuary. As well
they might. The dry-stone walls were strong,
and it was—or had been—the house of their God.

The beast flowed closer. Its curves held terrible grace and power. Belly-plates churned the
soft earth over the graveyard. They lay shallowly
buried, the olden monks. Behind the serpent a

shrivelled arm pointed at the sky. And still it came.

All of it was out of water now. The finlike crest along the chine gleamed sharp; the tapering tail whisked the ground. Brigit no longer held its attention. It passed her by. She turned to watch: the monster's head drew level with Ranulf's hut. Save for a distraction it might have gone on toward the chapel.

But somehow Ranulf had crawled to the doorway. Kneeling, he steadied himself on the frame. In his left hand he brandished his sword,

and he cried a defiance.

Brigit did not know if the creature heard or understood, but the great head turned, the eyes fixed on Ranulf, and the tongue flicked forth.

Ranulf swung his sword aloft. It gleamed sharp in the lightning-glare, but it wavered in his grasp, and against the serpent was flimsy as a withe.

"Stop!" Brigit screamed, and ran.

The monster saw her movement and turned toward her again. Its tongue darted out, inquiring. "Stop, Ranulf! A sword is nothing against

that!" She threw herself between Cata and the
hut. Alarmed, the beast arched its neck and
gaped its jaws. The mouth was huge; Brigit
could have stepped inside. From the upper jaw
gleamed two white fangs. Lesser teeth, sharp
and curved, glinted through darkness. Again the
tongue licked. This time it smeared across her
face. She screamed and backed away. Pearls of
liquid spattered from the fangs and pooled yellow on the ground. Where they touched water
they steamed.

Behind her, Ranulf cursed and tried to push
her aside. Brigit's foot slipped, and she went
down in mud. The serpent poised to strike.
Ranulf snarled a challenge.

She looked up at the grinning head and
cried, *"Hold!* It was I who called you in Brigit's
name. In the name of Mananaan Mac Lir who
answered, I command you, *hold!"* She struggled
to her feet and staggered forward. The head lowered. An eye glared at her. She took yet another
step, made a fist, and smote the muzzle once,
twice, thrice. The beast flinched back.

She heard a shout close by. Halldor stood in
the churchyard, pelting rocks. His left hand
gripped his sacrificial hammer. The creature
hissed and turned toward the annoyance.
Halldor retreated backward, a step at a time,
edging toward the high round tower.

The beast's front coil crushed gravestones and
crumbled crosses. It flickered a tongue toward
the chapel door. Halldor tossed another rock.
The creature slid toward him, angered.

"Halldor—" But Brigit could only croak.

"He lives, then," said Ranulf, behind her.

"He does that," Brigit whispered, "but for how long?" She lurched back into the doorway.

As it passed another wicker hut, the beast's tail curled. It ripped the door from its hinges, hooked around a doorpost, and, with splintering wood and men screaming, the hut crashed down. Another coil surged against the chapel wall, but the stones held firm. As Brigit and Ranulf watched, Halldor retreated toward the tower, Cata behind him.

 # XIII

Halldor had in mind to stand against the worm, as Thor will stand against Jormungandr at the Weird of the World. He bore no hope of winning over it, but he might—he barely might keep it in play long enough, even hurting it a little, that men would regain their wits and take shelter in the tower. There it could not reach them, and maybe it would not abide at the base until the food stored within was gone. Maybe some of them would have enough steadfastness toward their old skipper that they'd carry Ranulf along.

Through lancing rain and pelting hail, he saw young Lambi Hurtsson seized, slain, eaten. The rest had scattered every which way. Raising its wedge of a head, the troll fixed eyes on Halldor and began to glide near. Beneath wind-shriek he heard it hiss. Venom dripped thick and yellow from its fangs.

Then suddenly it veered. For several wild heartbeats he did not know why. A twist of the

man-high coils showed him Brigit. She'd been
hidden from him by that bulk. Now she fled, and
it followed. He remembered amidst the thunder
that snakes are drawn by the movement of prey.
"Hold still!" he shouted to her. The storm shred-
ded his words. Yet after fleeing, stumbling,
fleeing onward, she did halt. Like a post she
waited in her mired and soaked garb, and the
beast slithered on past her.

After another to-and-fro billowing of the vast
body, Halldor saw why. Ranulf stood in the door
of his hut, leaned against the jamb, feebly wav-
ing a sword in his left hand.

Halldor groaned. He started thither, to die
beside his boy. Or, no; as he tripped on a grave-
stone that the giant had knocked askew, the
thought flickered that he might gain its heed,
bring it back toward himself. Other stones lay
broken by the weight, in flinders that he could
throw.

But Brigit—Brigit was going to Ranulf! She
was defying the worm!

Bewilderment rocked Halldor's being. First he
had supposed she'd raised the thing herself in
avenging witchcraft. Surely her rede about
sailing around the island had been an ill one.
When it chased her, he had wondered in a flash
whether she might indeed be blameless. Last he
saw that she did have some kind of power over it
. . . though she was using that to save Ranulf,
whom she hated—

Meanwhile Halldor had been casting chunks
of crosses and chiseled words against those

glimmery scales. He had been howling curses and taunts. Baffled of the son, the dragon turned once more against the father.

And they had gotten so close to the tower that folk could withdraw there no more. Halldor would die for naught. Thereafter the troll would squirm about, feasting. Well, many old tales said that men who fell bravely would meet again at the board of the gods. Halldor had his doubts about that, but—

Lightning blazed from end to end of heaven. Thunder rolled, shaking the earth, like the wheels of a mighty wagon. Halldor caught his breath. His fingers closed tight around the hammerhaft. It was as if that flash had shown him what he could still do.

He whirled about and ran for the tower. It was terrible not to see how close behind his foe was. He heard only waterfall hiss and rasp of belly-plates over stones, squelp of mass through mud, ever more loud. Wind and rain were befouled with smells of snakeflesh and poison. He must not lose time by looking over his shoulder.

Ahead loomed the grey height. Strange, he thought in a hidden part of himself, strange and maybe just, that he who had rooted out the right-ful owners of this building, must seek it like a hunted animal.

The scaffold leading to the overhead doorway stood hard by the boulder where he had slain a horse to his gods. Rain had washed away the blood of that offering. In time, it would wear off the graven sign of the gods themselves. *But*, flickered through Halldor, *a man can only do whatever lies within his strength, in whatever span the Norns give him.* He scrambled up the frame and past the now empty entrance.

Beyond, the room was chill, dank and dark. The stones fended off much of the storm-racket outside. He stopped to gasp.

The scaffold crashed to bits before the snake. The height was not too great to get down from, but Halldor did not await that he would ever do it. Gloom thickened when the armored neck reared athwart the opening. The snout battered;

a shiver went through Halldor's footsoles. But the monks had wrought well. The tower was unscathed. The beast could not get more than the end of its muzzle inside.

Rankness stung Halldor's nostrils. He rallied his will. "Thor with me!" he roared, and swung the hammer. It crashed upon the plated mouth, iron head driven by a seaman's arm. Hissing seethed. Venom splashed. A drop struck Halldor on the wrist and burned like a hot coal. He smote at a fang, and saw chips fly off its bone whiteness.

Again. Again. The dragon withdrew. The room filled with storm-sky's grey, till lightning glared afresh. Halldor saw the gleam of it flame off the scales beyond. Thunder banged.

He must keep the worm here, mindful of none but him. Then maybe, maybe his folk could get to his ship and bear Ranulf to safety on the mainland. But if he stayed in this room, where he could not be caught, the hunter from the deeps would soon turn elsewhere. Besides, that crack of fire above the graveyard had kindled in him the littlest, wildest of hopes for himself, too—

A ladder leaned against the trap leading up to the next floor. Halldor swarmed aloft. He pulled the ladder after him, and so went onward. The higher he climbed, the more the gale was muffled, for here were naught but narrow windows. He heard echoes of his hasty footfalls and even his harsh breathing. It was as if the ghosts of the monks stirred in the murk around him.

He went on upward.

At the top, below the roof that turned against heaven like a shield boss, he must halt for breath. From mouth down into lungs, he blazed and withered. He drank gulp after gulp of the wet air of Ireland, and slowly his knees stopped shaking.

He went to the window and leaned out. At once the weather was everywhere about his head. Wind, rain, hail smote him in the face; it yowled, it roared, it seared. He laid hand above brow and squinted. The snake still writhed at the bottom of the tower; but he saw its neck weave back and

forth, in search of easier prey.

He must draw yonder unblinking eyes his
way. He shouted. The sound was lost. And had he
not heard that snakes are deaf?

The hammer—He got it past the stone frame
that squeezed him. His left hand clutched a
rough sill for steadiness. His right hand whirled
the hammer on high. When it had gathered
speed, he took aim and let go.

Earth, the mother of Thor, hauled it ever faster
downward. It dwindled in his ken, became a lost
speck.

It smote.

He could only see that it struck somewhere on
his head, for that jerked backward, down, up,
around. Jaws gaped, tongue flickered. "Here I
am!" he cried, and waved both arms to beckon.

The monster saw. It raised its lean skull,
higher, higher, until he made out—with a leap in
his breast—that his hammercast had split the
flesh. Blood ran forth, red across black, and
mingled with the rain.

The wound was not deep, but the beast was in
a Fimbul-cold rage. It could not reach him,
though it lifted so near that he whiffed once
more its venom. The head lowered, swung out of
his sight beyond the wall. It came back on the
other side.

The worm was coiling itself around the tower,
hitching itself up toward him.

Halldor felt a grin on his lips. This was as he
had wanted.

He must stay leaned out of the window, to

keep that dim mind aware of him. When the
dragon got this far, which would not be very
soon, he could duck inside. He could do his best
to anger it further; he had a sheath knife at his
belt, if nothing else. In the end, of course, when it
began to give up, he must go back to it and be
taken, to buy more time. Unless by then *Sea
Bear* had gotten clear. . . .

An odd peace waxed within him. The storm
that battered his upper body seemed far off.
Memory lifted and drifted, as if the one of Odin's
ravens which bears that name were hovering

nigh. The green hills of Thrandheim; the fjord-walls elsewhere in Norway that went sheer to the clouds; Father, Mother, sisters, brothers, kinfolk; Unn, the children who had lived and the children who had died, their house, their strivings together; Brigit, eldritch and lovely—

Startled, he spied the adder head coming around the tower again, no more than a yard below him.

He looked into lidless eyes, the maw underneath, the coils beyond: into death.

He raised his face heavenward and said, quite softly, "Thor, old friend, fare *you* ever well as long as the world may stand."

White-hot came the blaze. Halldor never heard the thunder, though it toned through the stones of tower and church. An unseen whiplash cast him backward, down on the floor and into the dark.

—He groped his way toward wakefulness. First he knew how hard the planks were on which he lay, and how he hurt in every inch of himself. Worst was his ears. They were full of blades, and they keened, and that was all he could hear.

Bit by bit, the shrilling faded away. At last he could sit up. He began to make out noises. They were dull. It crossed his mind that, while he'd surely recover most of his hearing, it would never be as sharp as it had been. Well, a man grows old.

When the ache in him had ebbed enough, he clambered to his feet and sought the window.

The wind had shifted; rain blew straight in. But it was a softer wind, a milder and hail-free rain. The day was brightening. The storm was almost over.

Halldor looked down. A smear of scorch zigzagged across the wall the monks had built. At its bottom, blackened, smoking, bereft of life, the snake sprawled.

He was still too dazed to feel more than a very quiet gladness. So the least of his hopes had come into being. Who knew how much was the work of a god, or of which god? Halldor the Weatherwise did not. He knew merely that lightning often smites whatever raises itself too high.

XIV

Brigit left Ranulf crouched in the hut. Of his babble she could only identify the repeated name of Christ. She walked to meet Halldor. The rain had softened to a fine mist; wind had died, so that the river could be heard lulling past. The air had grown warmer, and her garments smelled of drenched wool. Almost, this homey scent drowned out the rankness of the dead monster. Cata's corpse was yet no more than a deeper shadow beneath the phantomlike tower. Brigit drew near the chapel.

The Irish captives who had sought sanctuary there had begun to venture forth into the great stillness. Likewise Norsemen straggled into sight from the ends of the island whither they had fled, but they hung back, they shuffled and sidled, droop-headed. They had been afraid.

No fear showed on the face of the man who stood foremost among the Irish. Rather something cold and terrible. Sturdy, he was, red-headed, clad in the soiled rags of what had been a fine tunic: a freeman farmer, once well-to-do, such as Brigit had known all her life. She started when he hailed her. "Are you satisfied, Lochlannach's whore?"

"What?"

He spat on the ground before her. "So you're thinking we none of us saw? Think you we were too beaten down, too despairing of God to keep eyes in our heads? We watched. I know that you lay in the tent of the heathen chief. I saw you steal forth into the dark, and I remember tales of how holy Senan once cleansed this island of the very thing that you brought back. Eamon was my brother, you harlot. Was it your apostasy drove him to his death?"

Brigit flinched back, though he made no move toward her. Behind him others of the ragged band muttered. She stammered: "But you cannot be understanding! What I did—and I'm not sure just what that was—I did to help you, to drive away the invaders, avenge our slain, restore honor to our outraged. You would all have been sold into slavery!"

He clenched his fists. "You lay with the enemy. You did not make him force you, as our faithful women did. And you called on pagan powers, trafficked with the Devil—you, once a

bride of Christ!''

A woman stepped from behind him. A mantle covered her head, and her garment was mudstained. ''Your pagan lover slew my man,'' she said, ''then his men used me, and laughed when I fought them. What they did not take of our household goods they burned—and brought me here as captive!'' She threw back her cloak, loosed her hair, and sank to her knees. ''Upon you, Brigit, adulterous bride of Christ, I set the

widow's curse: May you find no peace in this
your native land. May the grass spurn you, the
stones turn against you, may you be cast from
every door, and may God Himself show you His
back!''

Brigit retreated, shuddering. The woman
pointed at her and rose from her knees. "So be
it." She covered her hair. Her fellow captives
stood and stared.

As the woman spoke, strength had drained
from Brigit. The Shannon breeze clawed her
face. The land burned like coals under her feet,
and the air choked her.

Tears were thick and bitter in her throat, but
somehow she could not shed them. In a mad way
there passed through her, *the snake, the great
snake, tons of it there must be. What can they do?
Carve it up and cast it in the river before it grows
too rotten? Or try to eat it, perhaps?* She began to
laugh. *Whatever happens, no man of the Church
will ever chronicle the heathen doings on this holy
isle. The great bones will be sunk in the river, and
later generations will forget. But oh, in the mean-
time, the* stink! She turned from her countrymen
and ran toward the tower.

At its base the serpent sprawled lightning-
blackened and dead. Halldor stood beside the
altar of his own god. Upon it he had laid the
hammer, still dark with blood; but he waited,
arms folded, quiet in his countenance.

"How fares my son?"

"He is unharmed." She halted before him and met his eyes. She said nothing about Ranulf's soul.

Halldor nodded. "I thought so. I feared the poison—" Brigit saw an angry red burn on his wrist. She knew herbs to heal it. A wry, weary grin made creases around his lips. "Aye, that was a dragon to match Fafnir, that you called up from the deeps, Brigit." He raised brows over sea-blue eyes. "You did that, did you not?"

Dumbly, she nodded and stood braced.

He sighed. "I can hardly blame you. Sorry I am to have lost my oath-brothers, yes, many good men." Pause. "But of course, to you they were foes who came from nowhere, men you'd never harmed yourself. This was no blood feud, it was war."

Slowly he reached toward her, until his right hand lay on her shoulder. "After a war is done," he murmured, "peace may be made."

She shivered, but her tone held steady, and she looked him full in the face. "What is it you are saying, then, Halldor?"

Again the sad smile crinkled his features. "I know not altogether what. Still—oh, I mourn my friends and followers who went down. I'll see to it that their families get a rightful share of the plunder that *Sea Bear* carries home. But . . .you may remember, I'd no need or wish to carry on this viking cruise of ill weird. I'd won enough. Only my oath bound me. Now I can take my son home."

Brigit stiffened. "And my countrymen, as well, to sell as slaves?"

Halldor looked a long while at her before he said, "No, that's not needful, if you don't wish it. Let them stay here—" a slight chuckle— "and clean up the wreckage and the carcass. There'll be folk along eventually to take them home."

"You can be . . . kind . . . in your own way, Halldor."

His grip upon her shoulders tightened. "I'll return you to your father's hall, if you like, and offer him alliance—" She began to tremble. "Why, Brigit, what's wrong?"

She must clench her teeth, and still the shaking would not stop until she drew close and laid her head on his breast. He put his arms about her. "I am cursed, damned from the land, named whore and apostate. Ireland itself is poisoned against me, and I can live here no longer!"

His clasp about her tightened. Gladness leaped in his words: "But you can have the freedom of Norway!"

"I can what?" She raised her head and looked at him again.

He drew back just a little, but held her waist. His gaze searched her for that which he could not altogether understand, and awe was in it. "Come with me," he offered slowly. "But only if you will, Brigit. If not, I'll take you to wherever in Ireland you want—somewhere you're not

known—for you've dealt with mighty Powers,
Brigit, and something of them must be in you
yet. But if you'd come with me—henceforward
I'd be no more than a peaceful trader, and the
luck that's in you would sail in my ships. You
. . . you would be honored in my household."
For a span he seemed almost frightened. "If you
will."

She regarded him in turn, and awe was in her
look as well. This was the man who had slain
Cata—Cata, whom even holy Senan had but
banished. There rose the same sudden wish in
her as in him. For a moment she looked away,
toward the rain and the green hills of Ireland.
Then she shrugged and took both his hands. "My
own land is banned to me," she said, "and I've
nowhere else to go." She tilted her head and
smiled a bit. "You and I, together, might do
much; look at what we did, striving apart.
And—Halldor, Halldor, I want to go with you!"

She dropped his hands and stepped back.
"One more thing," she said. "A charm, before we
sail—a true one, this time. By the sacred well
grows a rowan tree; a branch of that, woven into
the side of *Sea Bear*, will bring your voyage luck.
And it's the last thing I can give you from Ireland."

*   *   *   *

An iceberg slipped by, huge, grey-white beneath stars and northlights, breathing forth wraiths of cold. Skafloc's breath gusted frosty as he spoke: "Do you know what became of them, then, Mananaan?"

The sea god shrugged. "Their ship sailed safely home, and ever after. Word came of their later doings. They lived as happily as I suppose mortals may, until they died. They were not often unfriends. She was thought to be a strong spaewife, and many sought her counsel or her help. It's said she had a fierce temper, but a kind heart."

"Ranulf, the son—did he live?"

"He did, but he returned to Ireland and became a monk. So much for his father's hopes, though Brigit bore other sons and daughters."

"What, then, of the first child she was carrying?"

"Oh, yes, I know something of him. Whoever the father of that one was—Halldor always took the boy as his own—he became a mighty man in Norway. It's said he fathered Gunnhild, the queen of King Erik Blood-ax—"

Skafloc gripped the tiller hard. "The witch-queen?"

Mananaan nodded. "Yes. The same. Beware, my friend, of calling upon the unknown. The answer is apt to be endless."

Their boat sailed on into the dark.

HISTORICAL NOTES

THE IRISH:

I savored my whiskey and looked out at the wind-whipped River Shannon. On Scattery Island the round tower was clearly visible from the window of the Galleon Inn, a pub in Cappagh, near Kilrush, County Clare. The room was rich with turf smoke.

"Mr. Beezley," I said, holding out my glass for a refill, "what you need here is a good monster. It would help tourism."

"It would, that," he agreed, and poured a generous portion.

"You could line the walls with blurry photos, and then refuse to talk about it. Keep people curious. Start rumors."

"But that monster was a long time ago. Saint Senan banished him, you know." He smiled and patted the head of his huge black dog.

"Well, maybe it's time Cata came back." We sat in silence and gazed 3½ miles across the river.

Cata, the monster of Scattery Island, is "real." Legend holds that Saint Senan, after a dreadful fight, vanquished the beast and founded a monastery. Senan died in 544 A.D. Over the centuries Scattery has been conquered many times. The vikings raided it in 816 and 835 A.D. (the latter is the occasion of our story). Then they did not return for more than a hundred years. One cannot help wondering why, when the location was so strategic. They again occupied Scattery from 972 to 975, and it was then recaptured by Brian Ború, who died in 1014 at the Battle of Clontarf. In later years it was plundered by the English and Normans, and the monastery itself was destroyed in Elizabethan times. Relics of these various occupations yet stand; the round tower, however, dates from the time of the viking raids. The island has long been considered important for seafarers. It was customary for new boats to sail *deosol* (sunwise) around it, and a pebble taken from its beach was said to guard against shipwreck.

The River Shannon, in which Scattery is located, is the largest stream in Ireland. On its bank now stands Shannon International Airport, first stop for transatlantic jets. The Shannonside area—and indeed much of the West of Ireland—has been developed for tourism. Vari-

ous castles host "medieval" banquets and,
perhaps more authentically, folk-villages of the
last century and settlements of the early Iron
Age have been painstakingly restored or recon-
structed.

This story takes place long before any castles
were built in Ireland. The nearby Craggaunowen
Project, however, replicates an iron-age settle-
ment, and settlements of that same type were in
common use on the West Coast until the six-
teenth century. Huts were round, with high
thatched roofs. The walls were wicker-woven
and smeared with clay; the floors were bare
earth. Cooking took place in a separate struc-
ture, because of the danger of fire. The monks on
Scattery probably lived in such huts; the only
stone edifices at the time would have been the
small chapel and the round tower. Such towers
were built for reasons which remain obscure; it
is thought that they served as lookouts or as
places of refuge during raids. The one on Scattery, well-preserved, stands 120 feet high. Also at
the Craggaunowen Project is a ring-fort of the
same period: these *raths* were surrounded with a
rock-and-earth wall, and topped by a palisade of
sharpened wooden stakes not unlike the stock-
ades of the American Old West. The defensive
wall sheltered buildings and cattle-pens. At
Craggaunowen these have been rebuilt. To this
day the Irish countryside is ringed with remains
of these ancient *raths*, though only the stones
survive. Souterrains—underground passages

beneath the walls—served as places of refuge, storerooms, and secret exits. It is probably such a fort that Halldor and his men attacked on their raid upriver, when they brought back Eamon as a slave.

Ireland in the ninth century was chaos. Not only was there constant danger from the marauding vikings, but native chieftains waged war on each other in a bewildering pattern of shifting alliances. Even monasteries would raid neighboring Church establishments.

We have striven to be historically accurate as far as possible. Our thanks to Jerry Pournelle for help with one technical point. As for others, in ninth century Ireland the lay clergy (priests not associated with a monastic order) were free to marry, as Father Eamon did. Monasteries were the repositories of books, and the clergy were the literate class. The medical procedure of trephining—cutting a hole in the skull to relieve pressure on the brain—was known even to the ancient Irish, so it is not unlikely that Brigit was aware of the practice: Irish physicians of the time also performed suturing and ligature of blood vessels. Convents and monasteries often served as hospitals.

A few Irish words may trip or confuse the reader. For those who are interested, then, here are explanations: a *geas* (pronounced gaysh) is a supernatural injunction, a taboo if you like, which renders otherwise morally-neutral acts forbidden. Such *geasa* (gesha) could be applied to one person, or to a position: for instance, the King of Tara was forbidden, when at Tara, to lie abed after sunrise.

The *Sídhe* (shee) are the faerie-folk and/or ancient gods of Ireland. *Samhain* (sow-ween'), the Celtic New Year, is October 31st. *Bealtaine* (Beltane) is May 1st. Many activities, such as sailing, are traditionally unlucky on that day. Brigit's observances (and she was trying for ill-luck), such as drawing and discarding first water, taking fire from the house, and having Halldor sail around Scattery, are all pagan survivals rooted in Irish folklore. Much later than the ninth century the old ways remained strong in the minds of the countryfolk, and they have, to this day, left their characteristic stamp on Irish Christianity.

A *gealt* (galt) is something like a Celtic berserker. In the heat of battle he is taken up with frenzy and eventually sprouts feathers and runs screaming through the treetops. Wandering for years, he finds his way to Glen na Gealt on the Dingle Peninsula and drinks from the water there. After he rests for a time in the valley his wits will be restored. This legend, with its overtones of manic-depressive psychosis, has caused me to wonder whether the springs in Glen na Gealt have a high lithium ion content. When last I checked the water it had, alas, been raining heavily for days, so accurate chemical analysis was impossible.

I admit one conscious point of historical inauthenticity. There exists a tenth-century description of Cata, the monster of Scattery Island, that bears no resemblance to the large serpent encountered in these pages. The beast was utterly fantastical and lacked elegance—though not halitosis. At a distance of four centuries, however, who is to say whether the medieval chronicler was correct? Besides, I am far more familiar with large snakes than with dragons: two huge healthy boas grace my living room. Otherwise, aside from historical or legendary "facts," which both my collaborator and I have tried to keep accurate, everything in this story is wholly fictional.

Mildred Downey Broxon

THE NORSE

No such people as the Vikings ever existed, and the word should no more be capitalized than should "pirate." One may speak of the viking era in the same way as of the era of the crusades—and about as misleadingly. By no means did everybody go crusading during the latter centuries; nor was everybody a viking in the former period. Indeed, full-time vikings were rather rare.

Then what did really happen?

The period lasted some three hundred years. The first recorded raids on England and Ireland took place in the late eighth century. From small beginnings, the movement soon gained such size, scope, and ferocity that a new line appeared in the litanies of Western Europe: *A furore Normannorum libera nos, Domine:* "From the fury of the Northmen deliver us, O Lord." The British Isles, France, Germany, and the Low Countries were ravaged over and over. In 845, both Paris and Hamburg fell to attack. At least one expedition fared down the Iberian coast and through the Mediterranean, plundering as it went. Finns, Lapps, and Balts suffered as much, though they had nobody among them at the time who could chronicle their woes.

These raiders were from Scandinavia, the area now occupied by the peaceful nations Denmark, Norway, and Sweden; later on, their colonies in Iceland and elsewhere furnished many. At a time when Western Christendom was divided among largely ineffectual kings and recalcitrant barons, the heathen Scandinavians came forth with vigor, discipline, excellent weapons, and the finest ships in the world. Population pressure must have been a driving force, for those are not lands that nature has richly endowed. However, ambition, greed, and adventurousness were surely just as strong. So, often, was the people's own quarrelsomeness. A man who got in trouble could gather a crew and take off overseas in hopes of mending his fortunes.

More commonly, a neighborhood band of yeomen would take ship together after the crops were planted, to spend a season as buccaneers.

They usually tried to return by harvest time.

Such a raider bore the name of "viking." The origin of the word is not quite certain, but probably it comes from "*vik*," meaning a narrow bay (cognate with Scots "wick"). A viking was, then, at first a "vik-ing," a man of the bay. He pronounced it to rhyme more or less with English "seeking." He and his bully boys lurked in an inlet. When a cargo vessel passed by, they pounced on her.

As kings and jarls—aristocrats—gained strength, such robberies became increasingly dangerous close to home. A lord was all too apt to hunt down the pests and slay them. But meanwhile ships had improved until they could readily fare overseas. Nobody objected to raids upon foreigners, and the pickings there were much better. Soon huge fleets went forth. They might be gone for more than a single year, their crews wintering abroad in order to get an early start come spring.

Frequently men found they liked it better where they were than they had done in their native countries. They settled down. In due course, colonization rather than plunder became the main purpose of Scandinavian warfare. The formidable armies that followed such leaders as Guthorm ("Guthrum"), Hrolf ("Rollo"), and Svein ("Sweyn") Forkbeard cannot be called vikings, nor can the settlers who moved in after they had secured the territory.

English writers down to the present day have

generally referred to the invaders as Danes. This
is only correct as regards their own country and
Normandy, where most, if not all, of the new-
comers do appear to have stemmed from the
general area of what is now Denmark. In Scotland, Ireland, and the surrounding islands, the
bulk of them were from what is now Norway.
Swedish enterprise abroad seems to have been
mainly directed toward Russia, and perhaps less
warlike.

Irish chroniclers drew a distinction between
"light" and "dark" breeds of Scandinavians.
The reference may be to Danes and Norwegians
respectively. The Irish name for Norway was
Lochlann, probably a Celtic-Nordic hybrid
meaning "coastal district," and the Norsemen
they called Lochlannach.

The history of these folk at home during the
viking era is equally turbulent. Here it is enough
to say that a strong Danish monarchy appeared
sometime in the late eighth or early ninth century, quite likely in response to a Carolingian
threat. At the time of our story, 835 A.D., Norway
had not yet been unified, but consisted of nu-
merous independent kingdoms and jarldoms.
Thrandheim, from which the modern city
Trondheim takes its name, was one of these. The
environs are not rugged like many other parts of
the country, but gently rolling.

So much for the dry outward facts. Can we
understand the people behind them, neither as
glamorous nor as bestial, but as human?

It is true that the vikings were cruel, rapacious, and wantonly destructive. Yet they were no worse in this respect than Christians; that would have been difficult. Only consider Charlemagne's massacres among the Saxons or, at later dates, William the Conqueror's depopulation of rebellious northern England and the horrors of the First Crusade. The vikings in their day were simply the most successful predators, and that largely by default.

Furthermore, as I have observed earlier, not all or even most Scandinavian men went in viking (to translate literally their own term, *gangu i víking*). Treasure is good, but you cannot eat it or use it for a tool. The majority by far must have been reasonably peaceful farmers, fishers, hunters, artisans, and the like. As for goods from abroad, traders must have handled more than vikings ever did. Such large, prosperous mercantile communities as Hedeby, Birka, Kaupang, and Gotland attest to this. Archeology shows that the network of trade reached through Russia as far as Constantinople and the Caspian Sea; southwesterly it linked itself to the Arab dominions.

We have tried to show Halldor as a small-scale yeoman-entrepreneur, forced by misfortune and against his will to turn viking for a while. At the same time, of course, we have not wished to sentimentalize him. It was a brutal age.

Though the Norse in Ireland destroyed a great deal, the Irish themselves had often done the same in their internecine wars. To that pastoral island the strangers brought innovations which included coined money, foreign commerce, and towns. If many took captives back with them, many others settled down and became a solid part of the folk. Thus it is no surprise that at the battle of Clontarf there were Celtic and Nordic warriors on both sides, and that, though BrianBorú died victorious on the field, no expulsion of foreigners followed. Ireland and the Irish have a way of winning love.

The pagan Scandinavians had a culture of their own, alien to Christendom but rich in its way. Besides such stunningly beautiful creations as the Gokstad and Oseberg ships, it brought forth much that is fine in art and well-wrought implements. Via descendants who wrote them down, it gave us the splendid literature of Eddas and sagas. If fierce toward enemies or victims, its men were utterly loyal to kin, friends, chieftains; nothing was more loathed than a betrayer or perjurer. Its women enjoyed a status that, once it was lost in the medieval period, they would not regain until the late nineteenth century. An almost religious respect for the law pervaded it; sometimes this became legalistic nitpicking, for these were a litigious people, but violation of the letter meant outlawry. Mostly freeholders, the population cherished their rights and liberties; for many generations they curbed their kings, and in Iceland they founded a unique sort of republic.

They had no prescribed faith. Individual beliefs and local practices ranged from the crudest superstition or the most barbaric rites—even human sacrifice—to concepts which had a certain splendor. Ideas about what lies beyond the grave were just as variable, often inchoate. Like other pagans, the Scandinavians were tolerant of different creeds and apt to borrow from them. If a single spirit can be said to have prevailed, it was that of courage in the face of doom. A man's death was predestined, but he could meet it in such a way as to leave an honorable name behind him. At the end of the world, the gods themselves must perish likewise.

There is much more to say, but there are also plenty of books to say it, if you are interested. Let me just remark on a few details pertinent to this story. Modern artistic conventions notwithstanding, warriors wore no wings or horns on their helmets; shields were rather small wooden discs, equipped with hand-grips rather than straps; men rode horses when they could, but always dismounted to fight; several distinct types of ship existed; merchantmen generally depended on sail alone, warcraft on oars unless the wind was right; by poling out a sail, though, a vessel—at least of the former, deep-hulled sort—could point fairly close; only the latter bore figureheads, and not always they; law required that these images be demountable, to take down when approaching a friendly shore.

As for the aftermath: In 872, at the battle of Hafrsfjord, King Harald Fairhair completed his forcible unification of Norway. The colonization of Iceland followed, by persons unhappy with his stern rule. Harald died old; his first successor was a son of his, Eirik Blood-Ax. That nickname is suggestive, yet according to the sagas, while he lived he was mainly guided by his wife, Gunnhild. Of her it is written that she was the daughter of one Ozur, a magnate in the northerly district of Hálogaland. We know nothing else about him, but he could well have moved up that way from Thrandheim. Gunnhild soon gained a sinister reputation as a troublemaker and, it was whispered, a witch. The story of her life is long and fascinating.

Denmark officially became Christian in the middle tenth century, Norway in the early eleventh, Sweden later still. Scandinavians continued to sail widely for some while afterward—as far as America—but only a few in viking, and they not for long. This was less because of their conversion than because the Western nations had grown too strong for them. The last Norse attack on Ireland was by King Magnus Barefoot, who fell there in 1103. When his son Sigurd took a fleet to the Holy Land, 1108–1110, and King Valdemar I of Denmark conquered the pagan Wends, 1169, they went as crusaders.

Poul Anderson